Philly Girl

Philly Girl

Marcus Weber

www.urbanbooks.net

Urban Books, LLC
300 Farmingdale Road, NY-Route 109
Farmingdale, NY 11735

ISBN 13: 978-1-64556-279-5
ISBN 10: 1-64556-279-4

First Mass Market Printing January 2022
First Trade Paperback Printing September 2021
Printed in the United States of America

10 9 8 7 6 5 4 3 2 1

Distributed by Kensington Publishing Corp.
Submit Orders to:
Customer Service
400 Hahn Road
Westminster, MD 21157-4627
Phone: 1-800-733-3000
Fax: 1-800-659-2436

Philly Girl

by

Marcus Weber

Chapter 1

"So are you going to the prom or what? And don't give me any of that shit about you not having a date, neither."

Sarita didn't hear a word her best friend, Shay, had said. At that moment, all Sarita's attention was focused on Nasir, who was being dropped off at school by his dad. Every time Hassan brought Nasir to school, it was like a car show. One day it was a Benz, the next a Range Rover. One week during the beginning of the school year, Hassan switched cars every day of the week. He wanted to make sure his son was going to be in the popular crowd.

"Baby girl!" Shay yelled while snapping her fingers in front of Sarita's face to snap her out of the daze she was in.

"I told you, girl, for the tenth time, I'm not going!" Sarita snapped back.

Shay had been bothering her about the prom all weekend. Sarita didn't want to tell her the real reason she didn't want to go, so she snapped at her to end the badgering.

"Wassup, baby girl? Wassup, Shay?" Nasir greeted them when he walked up to the girls.

Sarita was smiling from ear to ear. She was goofy in love with this boy. "Hey, Nasir," she giggled.

Shay spoke too but shook her head and rolled her eyes at her best friend. When it came to Nasir, Sarita was open and would do just about anything for him. Not only was he handsome, but he had a nice body, too. Nasir was tall and chocolate with naturally curly hair. That was why Sarita made him her boyfriend the moment she had a chance to.

"Sarita, I need to holla at you about something," Nasir said while gently pulling her away from Shay. "We'll be right back, Shay."

"To hell wit' y'all two!" Shay smiled, waving the both of them off.

"I was wondering if you wanted to go to the prom. I know I told you that I wasn't going, but I don't have to worry about SATs anymore. Kentucky offered me a full ride as long as I play ball for them."

Nasir was gifted when it came to basketball. He was six feet two inches and could outjump the gym. He was ranked as one of the top five players in the country. Scouts from all over had their eyes on him.

"Damn, Na! That's amazing!" She hugged him. "And you already know I'll go to prom with you."

"A'ight. I'll text you later so we can burn the mall down. And don't worry about ya wardrobe. I got you," Nasir assured her. He was well aware of Sarita's financial situation and wasn't about to leave that burden to her.

Nasir looked around and didn't care that there were a few teachers and students lingering in the hallways. Sarita was his baby, and he wanted the world to know it every chance he got. He leaned in and kissed her and held his lips against hers for a moment before pulling back.

Sarita couldn't help but smile as he gave a love tap on the side of her ass before walking off.

Hassan grabbed his phone from the center console and began to scroll through it, but in all actuality, he was looking through the rearview mirror at the black Impala two cars back that had been following him around all morning. "You niggas must think I'm slipping," he mumbled to himself as the light turned green.

Hassan wasn't just in the streets. He was also a major player in the city of Philly. He'd been a dope boy since the early nineties and controlled about 80 percent of the product being sold in the city, including cocaine. However, the hood had a funny way of showing him love. The scent of money brought the wolves out, and it was times like this he needed to be on point.

At the next red light, Hassan's suspicions were confirmed when the black Impala pulled up next to him. Two black males wearing black hoodies definitely didn't look like the police. "Go ahead and jump out there!" Hassan said, grabbing hold of the seventeen-shot .45 sitting on his lap.

He had a little more than $100,000 in the car and was about to protect it with his life. He could see the blitz coming like he was Tom Brady, and sure enough, right before the light turned green, the passenger- and driver-side doors of the Impala opened up. The passenger had an assault rifle while the driver had a Glock-like handgun. Seeing that, Hassan didn't hesitate to let bullets fly.

Pop! Pop! Pop! Pop! Pop!

All five shots blasted through Hassan's passenger-side window in the direction of the would-be stickup boys. Immediately the two gunmen retreated to their car, but not before sending a few projectiles Hassan's way.

As Hassan peeled through the red light, the gunmen took off through the busy intersection in pursuit. The traffic was so heavy that they almost caused two different accidents, but the drivers slammed on the brakes. Hassan dipped in and out of traffic. His adrenaline was pumping, and it wasn't until he looked into the rearview mirror that he realized the Impala wasn't behind him anymore.

He began to slow down, and everything seemed to be all right until he felt a burning sensation coming from his side. He looked down and saw the side of his yellow T-shirt covered in blood. He'd been shot. Instantly he felt woozy.

It was the usual when Sarita got home from school.

Her aunt was stretched out on the couch in her panties and bra, looking a hot mess. Sarita stood over her, looking down in disgust. Cocaine residue was all over the coffee table, along with an empty bottle of Grey Goose.

At one point in time, Sarita could remember when her aunt had it going on. For a white girl, Camille was country thick and had that black-girl swag, probably because she was raised in an all-black neighborhood.

About seven or eight years ago, Camille just lost herself. It was around the time when her sister, who was Sarita's mother, had died. She turned herself over to the bottle along with cocaine and partying just about every night. Her behavior was reckless and, at times, violent. The more family members tried to step in and help her, the more Camille pushed away and dove deeper into depression.

"Aunt Camille, I'm home," Sarita announced, still standing over her.

Camille cracked her eyes open after hearing Sarita's voice. "Clean this damn house. And don't take ya ass outside," Camille demanded. She didn't care that Sarita had assignments to do before her finals. She didn't care that Sarita had been in school all day and probably was a little tired. None of that mattered to Camille. In fact, having the house clean really didn't matter to her. It was just one of the many ways she oppressed Sarita and made her feel unwanted.

"Can you ask Isis to at least help me?" Sarita complained, but she was interrupted before Camille could answer her.

"Isis is not doin' shit!" Isis said, coming out of her room and fixing her hair. "Isis is on her way out the door."

"Dressed like that?" Sarita mumbled under her breath.

Isis looked like a hooker, and what she had on didn't make a lick of sense. The red skirt over her green leggings was just half the problem.

"You got something smart to say?" Isis asked, walking up to Sarita. She was both taller and heavier then Sarita.

Sarita didn't want any trouble. "No, not at all," Sarita replied with a fake smile on her face. She turned to walk off toward her room.

Isis reached out and grabbed a fistful of Sarita's hair, pulling her backward and putting her into a chokehold. If it weren't for Camille intervening, there was no telling where this would have gone.

"Let the little bitch go before she runs and tells her grandma on me," Camille spoke in a calm voice. "Just make sure you clean up this damn house like I told you to." She finished by leaning over and taking a line of the cocaine on the table straight up her nose.

Isis eventually let Sarita go, but not before she mugged her so hard that Sarita almost fell face-first into the bedroom door. It took everything in Sarita to not flip out. She probably would have given Isis a run for her money today, but instead she opted out. The prom was only a couple of weeks away, and scars on her face wouldn't have looked good in prom pictures. The only thing left for her to do was take a few minutes, let out a few tears, get herself together, and clean the house.

Dion walked into the emergency room, looking for her husband. After speaking to the nurse at the front desk, she was told where she could find him. She got to the little room he was in, and before she could cross the threshold, a detective came out of nowhere and stopped her.

"He's not allowed any visitors right now." The short and stocky black detective stuck his arm out.

Dion looked over his shoulder and could see Hassan sitting up in his bed with a bloody patch on his shoulder. She almost cried seeing him laid up in pain, but at the same time she had to transform into a lawyer and set aside her personal feelings. She reached into her bag and pulled out her credentials. "Is he under arrest?" She passed the detective her card.

The detective looked down at the card then back up to Dion. "He's charged with being a felon in possession of a firearm, possession of a firearm without a license, discharging a firearm in public, and reckless endangerment."

Dion looked over the detective's shoulder at Hassan, this time with a pissed look on her face. "Unless you feel like violating my client's Fifth and Sixth Amendment rights to counsel, I suggest you stand to the side," she warned the detective.

He did the right thing, stepping to the side. She made sure she slammed the door behind her so that he wouldn't be able to hear their conversation.

"What in the hell is going on, Hassan?"

"You know, when you're at the top, there's always gonna be someone who tries to take you down."

Dion shook her head, looking down at the handcuffs. It was times like this she wished her husband weren't in the game, at least, not as deep as he was anyway. Being that Hassan was at the top of the food chain, there was always somebody out there who wanted to kill him and/ or take his place.

"Damn, you look sexy when you're mad! Gimme a kiss!" Hassan joked, reaching out and grabbing Dion's ass with his free hand.

Dion pulled away but couldn't help but smile. She thought about how crazy her husband was even while lying in a hospital bed with handcuffs on.

"So how do it look?" Hassan asked.

Dion wasn't the best lawyer in the city, but she was no slouch, either. Having her own private practice gave her some flexibility, which in turn allowed her to fight a little harder for her clients. Every district attorney she battled in the courtroom respected her for that. They also knew they had to be on their A game at all times when dealing with her. Most of the time, the DA would rather work out a deal with her instead of going through the formalities of a trial.

"I'ma go and make a few calls and try to get the charges reduced. In the meantime, try to get some rest," Dion told Hassan before pulling out her phone and stepping out of the room. She didn't have a lot of juice, but she surely was going to use what she had for her husband.

Camille had nodded off for a few minutes but woke back up to see if Sarita had started cleaning the house. It was dead silent except for the sound of a few kids playing outside.

"Sarita!" she yelled as she looked around the house. It was the same as it was before she went to sleep. Clothes were still all over the place along with empty Chinese food containers and other pieces of trash. Dirty dishes were still in the kitchen sink, and the cat's litter box was starting to stink. Camille was mad as hell, even though she and Isis were the ones who caused the mess.

"Sarita!" Camille stormed down the hallway to Sarita's bedroom. "I thought I told your ass . . ." She stopped midsentence after pushing Sarita's door open and seeing that she wasn't there. "Sarita!" she yelled out again.

Sarita was nowhere to be found. Now Camille was really pissed and thought about all the painful ways she was going to discipline her. "Oh, this li'l bitch must have lost her mind!" she mumbled to herself. She tried calling

Sarita's phone, but it went straight to voicemail, only making things worse. This type of disobedience was not gonna be tolerated, and Camille had plans to deal with the situation just as soon as Sarita walked through the front door.

Little did she know that Sarita didn't have any plans whatsoever of stepping foot back in that apartment, nor the projects for that matter.

Chapter 2

Nasir looked over at Sarita, who was lying across his bed snacking on junk food and watching TV. Sarita was a dime all the way around the board, and Nasir didn't know how much more of her staying there he could take without trying to get some of her goodies. He never had sex with Sarita before, but he wanted to badly. Her period coming on the night before she got there really threw a monkey wrench in his game.

"So you just gonna lie there and eat Chocolate Juniors all day?" Nasir scooted closer to her on the bed.

Sarita rolled onto her back and playfully tried to feed Nasir some of the cake. "Why? You getting tired of me already?" she asked.

"Hell nah. You can stay here as long as you want."

Dion burst through the door, messing the whole mood up. "If they put out an AMBER Alert for you, ya ass is out of here!" she joked but was also serious.

"Ms. D, I'll be eighteen in a month," Sarita voiced. "Besides, my aunt don't care enough about me to do anything . . ." Sarita got quiet, thinking about her words. She used to have a good relationship with Camille, but things had changed for reasons she couldn't explain.

Dion could feel Sarita's pain. She couldn't understand how someone could be so mean to a child who was as beautiful and smart as Sarita. If Sarita weren't so ashamed of her aunt, Dion would have been able to reach out to her and give her a piece of her mind. Messing around with Sarita, Dion knew the chances of meeting Camille were slim to none, at least for now.

"So look, I'm about to go and pick up ya father. They gave him bail this morning," Dion told Nasir as she stood by the door. "That recruiter will be here at three p.m. sharp, so don't—"

"Mom, I know. I'll be ready," Nasir said, cutting her off.

The University of Kentucky had a scholarship waiting for him, but Duke was also interested in bringing Nasir over to their team. Dion was excited about that more than anything, and she wanted Nasir to attend Duke because that was where she'd graduated from. At this point, she wasn't about to let anything come between Nasir and his future. And although Sarita was cute and all, Dion was gonna make sure she got left behind as well if she didn't make it to college herself.

"I'm going to the mall when the recruiter comes," Sarita said.

"No, stay here. I want you to be with me."

"I think it's better if you do this alone. It's you they want, not me."

"But I want them to know we are a team. It's you and me."

"We are a team, but sometimes a leader needs to do it on his own. Besides, I need a prom dress." She smiled seductively.

Sarita wanted to give Nasir space for this possibly life-changing moment.

***

Before Sarita went downtown to shop, she decided to go over to her grandmother's house. Like always, Mrs. Scott was home. She was finishing up a meal.

"Hey, Grandma!" Sarita greeted her after Mr. George let her into the house. Having Mrs. Scott for a grandmother was the best thing that had happened to her. She was probably the only person in the family who showed her love.

"Now why are you over there looking like you just lost ya boyfriend? You need some money, baby?" Mrs. Scott asked.

Nasir had given her money already, so Sarita was good on that front. She had something else on her mind and wanted to get to the bottom of it before it killed her. "Grandma, I need to ask you something very important, and I'm begging you to tell me the truth," she began.

Mrs. Scott paused right in the middle of doing the dishes. She could hear the concern in Sarita's voice. She walked over and took a seat next to her on the kitchen stool. "Tell me, baby, what's on ya mind?"

Sarita took in a deep breath and was about to start crying thinking about Camille and Isis. "Grandma, why does my aunt hate me so much? What did I do to make her feel that way? Is it because I'm not a hundred percent white like most of the people in the family?"

Sarita and Isis were the only two people in the family who had color to them. Just about everybody else in the Scott family was white.

"No, no, no. It's not that," Mrs. Scott said, wrapping her arms around Sarita. Mrs. Scott grew up in North Philly near Kensington and Allegheny where blacks were more prevalent. She was far from the racist type.

However, the answer to Sarita's question was much deeper than that, and she wasn't sure if it was her place to tell, but at the same time she hated having to lie to her granddaughter.

"Sarita, I wanna tell you something, but before I do, you have to promise me that you understand that I love you very much," Mrs. Scott began. "Can you promise me that?"

Sarita nodded her head and fought back the tears that wanted to fill her eyes. She could feel that something hurtful was about to be said.

"When your mother was eighteen, she was raped by a guy named Darnell Johnson. Now I don't know all the facts to it, but I believe your Aunt Camille was there when it happened," Mrs. Scott explained, wiping the single tear that rolled down her cheek.

Sarita sat there stunned as she tried to process what her grandmother had just told her. "Wait! You say that to say what?" Sarita asked, looking at Mrs. Scott with curious eyes.

"Your mother's period came every month . . . She wanted to get an . . . We all thought . . ."

"Say it, Grandma! I wanna hear you say it!" Sarita snapped.

Mrs. Scott couldn't take any more. It had to be said or else it would eat her alive.

"Your father is the one who raped your mother, and that's the reason Camille feels the way she feels about you."

Mrs. Scott tried to reach out and place her hand on the side of Sarita's face, but Sarita smacked it away, not wanting to be touched. She sat there staring off into space as her brain continued to process the information. It was all starting to make sense. All the years of verbal and physical abuse she endured was the manifestation of a woman who was victimized.

"I have to go!" she said, getting up and grabbing her things.

Trying to stop Sarita from leaving was futile, and though there was much more to the story than what Mrs. Scott had explained, Sarita would have to wait for another time to hear it. Mrs. Scott simply put her head down and listened as Sarita left the house.

Hassan was brought out of the receiving room and had to sign a few papers in order to get his property. With him already being a convicted felon, his bail was sky high: $100,000.

Dion had paid the 10 percent of that bail with one of her credit cards like it was nothing. She gave Hassan a big kiss when he walked out into the lobby.

His arm was in a sling, but that didn't stop him from wrapping his arm around her waist. "These muthafuckas took my DNA," he reported.

"And they'd better have shown you a warrant for it, too."

A warrant was definitely issued being that there was blood all over Hassan's car. It was an active investigation, so Dion knew that she couldn't contest the warrant.

"So now what?" Hassan asked, looking for some type of direction as to what he should do.

Hassan's DNA was crucial to several other investigations, and as soon as they ran his DNA through the system, all types of skeletons were going to start falling out of the closet. One of the more serious crimes he was worried about being connected to was a murder, which had the potential to put him away for the rest of his life.

"Aside from this lingering over ya head, you need to find out who was trying to rob you," Dion said as they walked toward the car.

"If these niggas out here were bold enough to get at me in broad daylight, it must mean they were trying to kill me."

Hassan had a lot of niggas in the streets who loved him, but he had his fair share of enemies as well, one of them being SK, a major player in the game who had the north side of Philly on lock. Up until now, it didn't seem like SK would try his hand with Hassan, but money, power, and respect could change how any man felt. Hassan really wanted to see if SK was behind the attempt. If he was, then it was on.

Sarita didn't know how she got downtown. It was like she had been on autopilot, walking up and down the streets. Her thoughts were everywhere, and her feelings and emotions were scattered about. She even began to have suicidal thoughts, something she'd never had in her life.

"Sarita! Sarita!" somebody yelled from down the street. "Sarita!" she yelled again, walking across the street with her girlfriend by her side.

Sarita turned around, saw who it was, and kept walking without saying anything back to her.

That made Isis mad, and once she got close enough, she shoved Sarita from behind. "You think you grown, bitch?" Isis snapped, pushing Sarita from behind again.

Sarita got her balance, and with malice in her eyes she spoke. "Isis, you'd better leave me the fuck alone!" she snapped.

"Or what?" Isis shot back.

Onlookers passed by without interrupting, but they also watched as the confrontation unfolded.

"Isis, I'ma tell you one more time . . ." Sarita warned while balling up her fists.

Isis went to push Sarita again. Sarita cocked back and punched Isis in her face. Isis countered, and the two of them exchanged a round of punches.

Sarita had Isis up against a car, giving her the business. All the anger, all the pain, and all the confusion Sarita was feeling took over. She kicked and punched Isis to the ground, and once she was on the ground, Sarita continued beating on her.

Isis's friend wanted to help, but seeing how hard Sarita was going made her think twice about it. A cop on foot patrol saw the ruckus and darted up the street.

Sarita blacked out and grabbed the closest thing to her, which was a bottle.

"Get her off me! Get her off me!" Isis yelled, holding her hands out to try to stop the assault.

Craaack!

Sarita knocked Isis over the head with the Corona bottle, splitting her forehead wide open. The bottle broke, and just as Sarita raised a jagged piece of glass to stab Isis, the police officer dove in and grabbed Sarita before she could strike her. Blood covered Isis's face, and she was pretty much out of it.

"Get da fuck off me! Get the fuck off me!" Sarita yelled at the officer, who was placing her in handcuffs.

As her rage began to subside, Sarita began to cry. Even this brutal fight couldn't take her mind off the information her grandmother told her earlier that day.

By the time Isis got some of the blood out of her eyes so she could see, Sarita was already in the back of the police cruiser being taken to jail.

Chapter 3

Hassan pulled out of the car lot in a brand-new Jaguar S-Type, paid for straight up. The police department still had the bloody, shot-up BMW, and as far as he was concerned, they could keep it. His money was longer than two football fields, so it really didn't mean anything to him.

"So what it do, my nigga?" Hassan's boy Chuck asked from the passenger side. He knew that if there was an attempt on Hassan's life, they were about to handle it.

"We gon' slide through the projects and see what's good wit' da nigga SK. If he acts like he wants some smoke, we gon' light dat shit up!" Hassan responded while looking into the rearview mirror.

The two SUVs that were following close behind were his best shooters. They were the hyenas of the city. They'd shoot up anything anytime and anyplace, and they didn't give a damn about who they hit. Not only were they willing to kill for Hassan, but they were also ready to die for him.

"Strap up," he told Chuck as he pulled a compact .45 from under his seat.

Chuck reached down and grabbed the MAC-11 from under his seat, cocked a bullet into the chamber, and set it on his lap.

Hassan pulled into the Blumberg Projects, and instantly all eyes were on them. There had to be at least forty to fifty people standing out there, including a few children who were quickly taken away. From the moment Hassan and his crew got out of their cars, they heard guns cocking and saw dudes getting into strategic positions around the projects. It was so quiet that you could hear a mouse piss on cotton.

SK emerged from one of the apartments with two of his boys by his side. He had on a pair of blue jeans, white Airforce Ones, and a white Polo V-neck T-shirt. The obvious bulge at his waistline was none other than a .50-caliber Desert Eagle. He walked out and stood right in front of Hassan's car, rubbing his hands together.

Hassan had his arm outside of his sling, but SK had gotten the word that Hassan had been shot. "So let me guess. You came up in here with all this heavy artillery thinking that I had something to do with you getting shot," SK spoke.

"So wassup? I'm here right now," Hassan shot back while holding his hands up.

SK chuckled at the gesture, then looked over at Hassan's car. "Nigga, you know me better than anybody out here. If I wanted you dead, do you honestly think you'd be standing here right now? When I get at a nigga, I don't miss," SK said, looking into Hassan's eyes.

Hassan and SK had history, and after thinking about it for a moment, it made a lot of sense. SK never had a problem putting in his own work, nor was he the sloppy type. He probably had more bodies under his belt than anybody in the city. Hassan could easily take SK off his suspect list. But the fact remained that he just came up in SK's projects with guns out, and that was a no-no.

"My bad, cuz. Shit's crazy out here," Hassan said. He looked over at his crew and gave them a nod to turn it down.

"Yeah, I see, but don't bring that shit out here. This is the type of shit that'll get you killed. Now get up out of my projects 'fore shit gets ugly," SK concluded.

Hassan didn't like the way he was being talked to, but it was something he had to swallow for the greater good of his crew making it out of there alive. It would be a tragedy for them to go to war over a misunderstanding.

Hassan and his boys got back into their cars and respectfully drove out of the projects without further incident.

SK watched and waited until they were gone. Then he went back into the apartment where he had come from.

The projects went right back to normal operations like nothing ever happened.

Though Sarita was a juvenile, she was charged as an adult and was given $5,000 bail. Isis wasn't off the hook either, having been charged with assault as well. She had bail set at $2,500.

"Channel Thompkins!" an officer yelled out as he walked by the holding cell.

Sarita put her head down knowing that wasn't her.

"One of you girls done made bail," the officer said, looking down at his paperwork. "Who is Channel Thompkins?" he asked, looking up to see which one of them would answer.

"That's me!" Isis yelled while banging on the thick glass.

Instead of opening the door right away, the officer waved Camille to the back of the holding cell. Sarita wasn't surprised that the first door Camille stopped by was Isis's.

"Are you okay?" Camille asked her, seeing the one-inch cut to her head.

Isis affirmed that she was all right.

Camille then walked over and stood at Sarita's door. She shook her head with anger written all over her face. "Your ass is gonna stay here!" she yelled while pointing at Sarita through the glass. "Do you see what you've done to ya cousin's face? You're evil, and I'm not bailing you out!" Camille then rolled her eyes and walked away from the door.

Sarita watched as Camille led her daughter to the front, and she started to cry, but then she wiped her tears away and took a seat on the cold bunk.

It couldn't have been more than ten minutes before the officer came back to the holding cells and unlocked Sarita's door. "Come on. You made bail too," he told her.

Sarita didn't count on Camille to bail her out, so her only phone call went straight to Nasir. She knew for a fact that he was coming to get her, and sure enough, she walked out to the front and there he was, standing there with a smile on his face.

"You good?" he asked, wrapping her up in his arms and kissing her on the forehead. "This shit is all over YouTube," he chuckled as they headed out of the station.

Sarita didn't even get a chance to respond when she ran into Isis and Camille standing out front waiting for a ride. Nasir had Hassan's silver Range Rover sitting curbside a few yards away from them.

As Sarita walked by her aunt, she stopped, faced her, and looked right into her eyes. There was a moment when Sarita wanted to swing on her aunt and give her the business just like she did to Isis. She definitely had enough anger built up inside for the challenge.

Camille could see it, too.

Instead of going through with it, Sarita just walked off and got into the Range Rover, leaving Camille and Isis standing there looking stupid. They watched as the Range Rover pulled off from the police station.

Camille didn't know what part of this whole situation was the worst: Sarita beating the hell out of her daughter, or that Sarita had made the $5,000 bail and pulled off in a Range Rover. In any event, Camille was feeling some type of way, and the ride home was going to be silent.

Hassan drove in silence the entire way back to West Philly. His thought process was everywhere, trying to figure out who the two guys were who'd tried to bring him the move. Truth was, he'd done so much dirt in his day that it could have been anybody.

"Look, my nigga. We gon' keep a shooter wit' you at all times. If those niggas try to pull a stunt like that again, it'll be their last," Chuck said.

Hassan didn't feel any safer, but unfortunately he couldn't waste too much time on the matter. Aside from having a drug organization to run, he also had some legal businesses to operate.

"I'm gonna need you to make the pickup tomorrow. I'm probably gonna be in court," he told Chuck. "It's a lot of product, my nigga. You think you can handle it?"

"No doubt. Whatever you need, I got you, big bro."

"Good. I'll bring the bread to the spot tonight. No weed, no drink, and no fuckin' around tonight. I want you on point and focused for this drop."

This would be the first time Hassan would send anybody else to do business with his connect. If there was anybody he could trust to do what needed to be done, it would be Chuck. They had been together since grade school and had been through the mud coming up. This was definitely one of those times Hassan needed his boy, because after this score, Hassan's supplier wasn't going to be back in the States for a while.

Detective White sat at his desk looking over Hassan's case file. The preliminary hearing was tomorrow, and before he got into the courtroom he wanted the DNA report in his possession. Detective White was more than just familiar with Hassan. He'd watched him grow up in the streets of Philly. He alone had arrested Hassan at least a dozen times for crimes ranging from low-level drug deals to murder, but for every case he'd had, either he was beaten at trial or Hassan had pled out for a reduced sentence.

Hassan had made out on all his cases except for a vicious murder-and-assault case almost two decades ago. Key evidence in that case was excluded because it was obtained illegally. Without it, the DA had no other option but to dismiss the charges with prejudice, meaning they could pick the case back up at any time if some new and helpful evidence became available. The thing about a murder case is that there is no statute of limitations on it. Detective White had been depending on that for years and had a feeling that one day Hassan would mess up and give him everything he needed to charge him with the murder. Getting shot and bleeding all over the place was the worst thing Hassan could have done.

Chapter 4

Camille banged on her mother's front door like she was the police coming to serve a search warrant. Not surprised at all, Mrs. Scott knew who it was. In fact, she was expecting Camille to come and speak her mind about the conversation she and Sarita had.

"You had no right to do that!" Camille yelled the moment Mrs. Scott opened the door. "That wasn't your place!" she snapped, storming past her mother into the house.

Mrs. Scott wasn't the type to bite her tongue, especially with her own child. "So what, Camille? You planned on keeping this—"

"I planned on doing whatever the fuck I wanted to! That's my child!"

Mrs. Scott ran over and grabbed Camille's face and covered her mouth. "Shut up! Shut up!" she yelled back while pointing upward to let Camille know that Sarita was upstairs. She really didn't want Sarita to hear any of this conversation because she only told her part of the truth about why Camille didn't like her. Another thing was that Mrs. Scott wasn't going to tolerate any disrespect, not from Camille or anybody else. "Sit ya narrow ass down!" she demanded through clenched teeth.

Camille hesitated at first, but her manners began to kick in when she saw her mother getting upset. She took a seat on the couch, pouting with her arms crossed like she was a little kid.

Mrs. Scott made sure that she spoke in a low tone so Sarita couldn't hear the conversation. "Yes, I told Sarita about Darnell, but she was going to find out eventually. And why do you treat that girl the way you do? She tells me how you and Isis act toward her. You should be ashamed—"

"Ashamed? Ashamed?" Camille asked with her face twisted up. She jumped up from the couch, also speaking in a low tone. "Let's not forget that I wanted to get an abortion, but you didn't want me to."

"That was your baby, Camille."

"I didn't want her. Her father raped me, you dumb bitch!"

Mrs. Scott's hand reacted on its own, striking Camille across the face with plenty of force behind it.

"I don't care! I don't care," Camille cried out. "You wanted that baby—"

Mrs. Scott covered Camille's mouth again to quiet her.

The tears poured out of Camille's eyes. This was the first time she had ever broken down about the situation. She'd been holding back these feelings for years, only to take her frustrations out on the closest person to Darnell, who happened to be Sarita.

Seeing the hurt Camille was going through, Mrs. Scott started to feel a little guilty. "Baby, I'm sorry you had to go through what you did. And I know you might not want to hear this, but Sarita didn't have anything to do with what happened to you. She's still your daughter and is probably the most innocent thing to come out of this whole situation," Mrs. Scott spoke softly. "She needs you more than anything now."

Camille wasn't enthused by her words. She had disliked Sarita for so many years that it blackened her heart. The type of love and care Mrs. Scott was talking about did not exist, and Camille wasn't going to try to force it. "I can't do this," she said, wiping the tears from her face. "The girl is your problem now," she concluded. She grabbed her bag off the couch and headed for the door.

Mrs. Scott grabbed her arm to stop her, but Camille yanked away and walked out of the house.

The whole house was silent, and Mrs. Scott found it hard to hold back her tears. She knew that her words—if Sarita heard her—would only make things worse. She walked up the stairs, and as soon as she got to the top, she dropped to her knees right next to Sarita, who was crying her eyes out.

Sarita had sat there listening to the conversation as much as she could and only got bits and pieces of it. But it was enough to cut Sarita deeply to know that Camille had absolutely no love for her. And it was at that very moment that Sarita gave up too.

Hassan stood outside the courtroom with Dion, waiting for his hearing to start. The proceeding was only for the purpose of pleading guilty or not guilty and then to set a trial date.

"Mr. Johnson!" someone called out, causing both Dion and Hassan to turn around.

Detective White and two other detectives walked up and stood before them. White had a piece of paper in his hand and stuck it out so Hassan could read it. "I have a warrant for your arrest!" he announced.

Dion snatched the paper from the detective's hand. "On what charges?" she asked, looking down at the paper. She saw the murder charge at the top of the paper, and immediately she sucked her teeth in frustration. By the time she looked up, Hassan was already in handcuffs. He had a look of disappointment on his face. Dion didn't even have to tell him what he was being charged with because he already knew.

"I'm on my way down to the police station," she told Hassan. "Don't worry, I'll have you out of there before the end of the day," she assured him.

Being that it was a homicide, that task would normally be impossible. However, Hassan was not your average Joe on the streets. Not only did he have plenty of money and a lot of influence in the neighborhood, but he also had Dion. He didn't have to say a word, and he didn't, for that matter, as he was being escorted down the hallway and onto the elevator. The one thing he could count on was his wife, who was going to do everything in her power to get him out of jail. For now, it was back to the Roundhouse police station, where he would endure more picture taking and fingerprinting.

Isis sat on the couch watching Camille run around the house getting dressed up for another night out on the town. A stitched-up forehead and a bruised face wouldn't look good in a pair of heels, so Isis was going to sit this one out.

"Damn, Mom! You look hot," Isis complimented her when Camille walked into the living room.

When Camille wanted to, she knew how to make her-self look like a million bucks. Dark blue Seven7 jeans showed off her thick, curvy hips and thick thighs, and a backless white top complemented the gold Christian Louboutin sandals on her feet. Her long, curly blond hair was draped over her shoulders, and even at the ripe age of 37, she needed not one layer of makeup. She still had her natural beauty.

"Don't wait up for me!" she joked, throwing her keys into her Louis Vuitton bag. After all that had happened today with her mom, all she wanted to do was let off some steam, and in the process she was hoping that she got drunk and high enough to get laid by any random guy.

Hassan's past finally caught up with him as he sat in a jail cell looking at the walls. The possibility of spending the rest of his life behind bars crept into his thoughts. He calculated the second-degree murder charge and first-degree assault charge, and it still came out to fifty to a hundred years in prison if he was found guilty.

On the other hand, there was only one person who could make that life sentence become reality, and it was imperative that he make sure that person didn't make it to the courtroom. Usually, money was the tool to use to make witnesses not show up. But in this case, money held no weight. Hassan wanted his witness dead so he'd never have to worry about the charges popping up down the line.

Club Push was doing what it did every Friday night, which was jumping. VIP was sold out, and the dance floor was jam-packed. Even the lobby of the club was at standing room only.

"Boss, everything is looking good. I had the bar stocked an hour ago, and we're almost done selling the good stuff," Bishop, the club's manager, said as he followed SK through the crowd of people.

Aside from being the second top drug dealer in the city, SK also had a number of legit businesses and was working on opening his third nightclub. This one consisted of two levels, two dance floors, fifteen VIP sections, two presidential sections, three bars, two kitchens, and a rooftop lounge. The club had had a five-star rating for the past two years and was somewhat of a celebrity magnet.

"So look, I've been thinking," Bishop said to SK as they entered his office. "I think now would be the best time to start pushing up on the west side. You know, ol' boy Hassan got pinched for a murder rap today."

SK lifted his head at the unexpected news.

"Yeah. So you know his whole operation is in jeopardy right now," Bishop continued.

The legal businesses were cool, and SK did make good money from them, but his heart was truly in the streets. He was hood-bound for real, meaning that it didn't matter how much legal money he made, he always felt like there was nothing like getting that dope-boy money. "I'm wit' the takeover, but we gotta do this shit smart," he said, getting up from his desk and walking over to the panoramic view of the club.

SK looked down at the partygoers dancing and having a good time while he thought about how he was going to go about expanding his drug empire. "I'm not gonna go into any details right now, but after the weekend we'll jump all over it," he told Bishop. "In the meantime, relax and try to have some fun." He then grabbed his keys off the desk and left the office. He still had some guests to entertain tonight and wanted to get to it.

Camille had heads turning when she walked into Club Push, and from the moment she walked through the door, she had eyes on her. She had to have been hit on at least three times. She shot everybody down, only being there to let off some steam.

"Can I have a rum and Coke?" Camille yelled to the bartender as she took a seat on a stool. She looked over at the dance floor and saw that everybody seemed to be having a good time. Nicki Minaj was blasting through the speakers. Feeling the music, she grabbed her drink and took it to the floor.

Camille's modest but sexy dancing caught the eyes of SK. He couldn't help but notice her. White chicks weren't really his thing, but for one who looked as good as Camille, he was about to make an exception.

Camille kept dancing with her cup raised up in the air when the music was shut off. Everybody stopped dancing and began to look around the club. SK jumped down off the DJ booth and walked over to Camille. She had a confused look on her face, not knowing who SK was and why he was walking up to her.

"Did you turn off the music?" she asked SK. The people who were standing around also had confused looks on their faces.

"You damn right I turned off the music!" SK shot back.

"Why?" she asked, looking around the room with all eyes on her.

"'Cause I wanted to talk to you without having to shout over the music. So let me ask you this: do you have someone special in ya life?"

"Oh, my God! I can't believe you! Are you serious?" she asked, her cheeks blushing. "Can you at least turn the music back on?"

"Only if you agree to come with me to a quieter place."

The crowd burst out in a chant, telling Camille to, "Go! Go! Go!"

"Okay! Okay! Hurry up before these people kill us!" she said with a smile.

One wave to the DJ and the music was right back on. SK took Camille by the hand and led her to the rooftop where the music wasn't so loud.

Camille had been in this club dozens of times, and not once had she ever been up to the roof. It was mainly reserved for the upper class. The view of the city's skyline was amazing.

"Yo, let's cover the basics—your name, where you're from, ya relationship status . . ." SK began and pulled out a chair for Camille to sit in.

Camille declined, wanting to stand at the roof's edge to take in the view. "My name is Camille, thirty-seven years young, got a daughter and no man. Got my own house, about to buy a car sometime next week, and I'm very good at pleasing myself. So tell me . . ."

"SK. My name is SK."

"So tell me, SK, what do you think you can offer me besides a few free drinks in ya club, probably dinner, and a hard dick?" Camille asked.

SK liked the way she talked. It was a relief to have someone be straight up the way she was. "Well, I'ma be honest wit' you. Hard dick and a few drinks was all I could come up wit'," he said in a joking manner.

They both shared a chuckle.

"Nah, I'm just messing wit' you. But on some real shit, I don't have game to spit or some fancy punchlines. I'm not trying to offer you the moon and the stars neither. All I wanna do is kick it wit' you, maybe go out sometime so I can get to know you."

"You don't wanna get to know me. If you do, you might not like what you see."

"I'm lovin' what I see!" SK shot back, looking into her eyes.

They both stood there looking into each other's eyes for a moment. In any other circumstance, the timing would have been right for a kiss, but SK passed up the opportunity.

This was the first time in a while Camille had entertained a man for this long, but it felt good. Plus, SK wasn't bad looking at all. She wasn't sure how far she was willing to let this play out, but for now just enjoying the rest of the night was going to be enough for her.

Hassan was able to see the night-court judge but was unable to get bail, The judge wasn't trying to hear any arguments from Dion, nor did he care to hear anything from the DA in this case. A preliminary hearing was set for Monday, in which the judge assigned to the case would determine whether Hassan would get bail.

"So what do you think is gonna happen on Monday?" Hassan asked, looking through the interview window at Dion.

"I think it looks good, considering you posted bail on this case before and made every court date without any problems."

This wasn't the real conversation he wanted to have with her right now. After reading the charges again, the disturbing details of this case seemed to be bothering Dion again, just as it did sixteen years ago. "What's wrong?" he asked, seeing the sad look in her eyes.

There wasn't enough time left in this legal visit for her to talk about what was going on in her mind. There were a lot of unanswered questions that needed to be addressed, but it was going to have to wait until another time, hopefully when Hassan got home. One thing was for sure—he was going to have all weekend to come clean about what really happened in this murder case.

Chapter 5

Nasir and Sarita strolled side by side in the mall, spending some much-needed time together before he went to basketball camp in North Carolina. The school year seemed to be coming to an end rather quickly, and within a month the summer would be here.

"Why are you so quiet? What are you thinking about?" Sarita asked before walking over to the water fountain and taking a seat on the edge.

Nasir did have a lot on his mind. "I was just thinking about you. I wanna go play ball, but I don't wanna leave you behind. North Carolina is far as hell," he said, shaking his head at the thought. "What if you could come with me? Would you come?"

"What are you talking about? I don't have that kind of money to just pick up and leave. And I damn sure won't allow ya folks to pay for my schooling, so you can get that out of ya head."

Nasir was more concerned about losing Sarita than anything else.

Sarita didn't want to be apart from him either. But she knew that if she asked him to stay or to go to a college that was closer to home, it would be selfish of her. She wasn't going to do that. Besides, her mental state wouldn't allow her to take on something so big as college right now. There were a lot of family secrets and issues that needed to be dealt with before anything else.

"If you're worried about me and you breaking up, then don't. We'll make it happen. I'll come visit you as much as I can. We can Skype and call each other every day. And when you come home for a break, we'll turn up," she said with a smile.

It sounded good, but Nasir had his doubts.

"Nasir, I'ma be here. Look at me," Sarita said, turning his head to face her. "I want—no—I need you to go out there and show those country boys how to play ball. Maybe, just maybe, you can take yo' ass to the NBA and move us far away from here."

Sarita didn't know it yet, but the words she just spoke had become Nasir's motivation to be the best basketball player he could be.

"Now come on. Let's go get our prom clothes before we end up putting it off for another couple of days," she said. She jumped up, grabbed his hand, and led him to the department stores.

SK walked into one of his trap houses and could smell the thick aroma of crack cocaine in the air. He walked into the kitchen where one of his workers was cooking up some powder.

The product was being whipped into the oils just the way SK wanted it. He hadn't cooked it himself in a long time, and just watching it being done made him want to take a stab at it just to see if he still had it. "Move over, li'l bro. Let me show you how a vet gets it in," he said, tapping the young kid on his arm. SK grabbed four and a half ounces and was about to drop it into the Pyrex pot, but he paused when Bishop came up the basement steps.

"My nigga, we gotta take care of dis shit!" Bishop said in an urgent manner.

SK got so caught up with wanting to cook the coke that he had forgotten the real reason he was there. "Don't touch this. I'm coming back up to finish," he told his worker.

Heading down the basement stairs, SK pulled the Glock 9 mm from his waistband. He knew that he was about to use it. "Damn, bro! What part of 'relax for the rest of the weekend' didn't you get? You gotta learn how to have fun in life," he playfully said while poking Bishop in his side with his finger.

Bishop wasn't the partying type, but he got the job done when it came to street business. That was one of the reasons SK had love for him, that and the fact that they were like family.

"Look at you two dumb mothafuckas!" SK said when he walked into the room. Sitting there with stupid looks on their faces were Bang and Dom, the two li'l homies Bishop had hired to kill Hassan.

"SK, my bad, bro! Just give me another day or two, and this shit will get done!" Bang pleaded.

"Yeah, man, that muthafucka got away once but—"

Pop! Pop!

Dom was silenced with two shots to his chest.

SK then turned the gun on Bang. "See, what you muthafuckas fail to realize is that I don't do second chances," he said while waving the gun in Bang's face.

Bang was scared to death now that he was about to be next. "SK, gimme a chance to fix dis!" he pleaded one last time.

SK looked over at Bishop, raised the gun up to Bang's head, and pulled the trigger, all the while looking Bishop in the eyes. The bullet hit Bang on the top of his head, taking a chunk out of it and knocking him backward.

"Get somebody down here to clean this shit up," SK told Bishop as he was leaving to head back upstairs.

Bishop took one look at the two bodies, then pulled out his phone to call his cleanup crew.

When SK got upstairs, he went into the kitchen and got back to cooking up the cocaine with his worker.

Giving Nasir some time to spend with his mother, Sarita decided to stop by Shay's house for a little while to catch up on the latest gossip.

"I know you better have that dress in that bag," Shay said when she opened the front door. "And when did you learn how to drive?" she asked, looking out at the white Chrysler 300 sitting in the driveway.

Sarita pushed past her and handed her a black shopping bag. "Nasir let me hold his car until he finishes having lunch with his mom." She flopped down on the couch.

Shay wasted no time unzipping the bag and pulling out the dress. "Oh, this is nice!" She held up a black Dolce & Gabbana dress with gold trim.

The dress cost $1,200, which Nasir didn't have a problem paying for. He also didn't mind paying $650 for some glitter and a pair of leather Christian Louboutin shoes to match the dress.

"You on ya grown woman shit wit' this!" Shay approved. "So did you let Nasir eat ya cookies yet?" she asked and flopped down on the couch next to Sarita.

"Not yet. I plan to, but I just got so much shit goin' on in my life right now. I haven't even been in the mood to be sexual."

"Girl, don't let that shit wit' ya aunt and ya crazy-ass cousin take over ya life. Outside of them, you still got a lot of people who love and care about you. If she don't want to claim this beautiful child as her family, then I know for sure my mom will." Shay smiled but was serious. She was a true friend indeed, and Sarita was grateful to have her in her life.

"Thanks, girl. You know I love you back," Sarita said, and leaned in for a hug. "But there is something that I need ya help with." She grabbed Shay by the arm and pulled her into the dining room, where the home computer was. Shay was a pro at finding people on the internet, along with their contact information.

"His name is Darnell Johnson. I think the nigga's from Philly too," Sarita told Shay, who began to type in the name.

"And this is supposed to be ya dad?"

Sarita got serious. "He's not my fuckin' dad! He's a creep who needs to be dead or in jail!" Sarita shot back.

Shay apologized, knowing how sensitive the situation was.

A little more than an hour went by before Shay felt like she locked in on the right person. In the city of Philadelphia, there had to be at least twenty-five people with the name Darnell Johnson. Fortunately for the girls, there was only one who fit the profile.

"I think this is him," Shay said, scooting over so Sarita could see the screen.

An article in a Philadelphia newspaper provided good information because Camille and Sarita's mom were listed as victims. Shay clicked on another page, and Darnell's picture popped up. He was black, had a stocky build, and had dreadlocks that fell down to his waist. She studied the picture before looking back at Sarita.

"What do you think?" Sarita asked.

Shay looked again, this time twisting her head to the side. "Dis nigga looks like he's Jamaican or some shit. I really can't tell though. He could be, but the dreads are throwing me off."

Shay checked to see if there were any other pictures of him, but there weren't. Darnell Johnson didn't have a Facebook page or Instagram or Twitter accounts. And according to the Department of Justice, he wasn't locked up by either the Feds or the State.

"Can you print me out a copy of that picture?" Sarita asked.

"Yeah, sure. But what are you planning on doing? And don't tell me, 'Nothing,' because I know you all too well."

Sarita sat there staring at Darnell's picture on the screen. She had so much anger and hostility built up in her heart for the man. It was because of him that her life was so hard. She wasn't going to lie to her best friend and really didn't know how she was going to take it. "I'm going to find and kill him."

"Yo, everything's a go on that situation. I got Tank and Styles going down North to holla at those niggas to see if they wanna get down wit' da takeover," Bishop informed SK.

SK leaned up against his car, looking up and down the street at the heavy crackhead traffic going in and out of one of his trap houses. He thought about how much of a power move it would be to have the west side on lockdown. West Philly and North Philly made the most money in the city when it came to the drug game, and he wanted to have his hands in everything.

"Let dem niggas know that I got it fo' da low over here. Dope, coke, weed, and whatever else they need," SK spoke.

SK's phone began to vibrate in his pocket, and when he looked down at the screen, he could see that it was Camille calling. "Damn! I was wondering if you was going to ever call me," he said when he answered his phone.

"Don't play, boy. What was wrong wit' you calling me? You got my number," Camille countered. She enjoyed the conversation they'd had the other night, and was feeling SK. She just didn't want to seem thirsty by calling him right away. "So I was wondering if you wanted to grab something to eat," she said, looking down at her watch.

"Yeah. What do you have in mind?"

"My place in about an hour. I can cook whatever you want . . . if it's food that you really want to eat!" she said seductively.

SK looked over at Bishop and stuck his hand out for some dap. Bishop smiled. He had seen that same look in his boy's eyes before. It was a look he had when he was chasing some pussy.

"I gotta shoot to the crib right quick and change my clothes. I been working all day. Just text me ya address, and I'll call you when I'm on my way. Do you need me to bring you anything?" SK asked politely.

"Just you and a couple of condoms!" Camille shot back.

SK grabbed a handful of his crotch, thinking about all the sexual things he was about to do to her. Being at her house in a New York minute was an understatement.

Cars honked their horns behind Sarita while she sat at the traffic light. The light was green, but she wasn't moving. Her thoughts were all over the place while she looked down at the printout pictures of Darnell.

"You dumb bitch! Drive!" a motorist yelled out after pulling up next to Sarita's car. His voice snapped her out of her train of thought.

Sarita couldn't believe some of the awful thoughts she had about watching Darnell take his last breath. It was pure evil from all those sleepless nights she had when she was beaten by Camille and all the extra beatings she got when she cried out for a dad she never knew.

Shay might have thought that Sarita was joking around when she said she was going to kill Darnell, but she was serious and was going to do it just as soon as she found him.

Camille raised her head from the coffee table after taking a line of cocaine. A knock at the door got her attention just as the high hit her. She sat back on the couch and wiped the powder from her nose. Another round of knocks on the door pretty much started to blow her high. She knew that it couldn't be SK because she hadn't texted him her address yet.

"Who is it?" she yelled and got up off the couch and walked to the front door. A quick peek through the peep-hole revealed that a white male was standing there. "Can I help you?" she asked, cracking the door open slightly.

Detective White flashed his badge. "I was the one who dealt with your and your sister's case back in '98."

"Oh, yeah, I remember you. What's going on?"

"Can I come in for a minute?" White asked.

Camille was about to let him in but then thought about the cocaine she had sitting on the coffee table. She squeezed out the door and closed it behind her. "I have company," she lied.

"Well, I just wanted to let you know that we've made an arrest in your case. We arrested Darnell Johnson," he explained. "There's a hearing coming up soon, and I was wondering if you still wanted to put the man who raped your sister behind bars."

Camille thought that she would be happy to hear the news, but that wasn't the case. It seemed like everything was happening all over again, just at the time in her life when she'd started to get over the situation. Thoughts of the events that took place that night made her become a little lightheaded.

"Ms. Scott?" the detective spoke, leaning in to see if she was all right.

Camille panicked for some odd reason. "I have to think about it," she said, and then turned around, entered her apartment, and slammed the door behind her, leaving the detective standing there.

SK got the text from Camille telling him to meet her at the gas station on the boulevard down the street from where she lived. Camille wasn't ready to reveal where she really lived just yet. Part of it was a little shame, being that she lived in the lower-class section of the city. The other reason was because she really didn't know him.

"Damn, you look even more beautiful in the light," SK said, watching Camille cross the street. Camille was rocking a floral sundress with her hair pulled into a ponytail. A pair of Gucci shades covered her eyes. "I thought you were going to cook for me," SK said with a smile.

"I changed my mind. How about we go to your place?" she said, placing her hand on his chest. "Unless you have a girlfriend and we're not supposed to be there," she added with a smile.

SK chuckled. The best thing about being a bachelor was that SK lived by himself. "Nah, no girlfriend over here," he chuckled. "Not yet anyway. I have to warn you, though, if you come to my place, you might not wanna leave."

Camille looked him in his eyes. "We'll see about that."

When SK pulled up to his home, Camille was impressed with his living situation. The four-bedroom, three-and-a-half-bath house fit his character to a T. Compared to the other houses on the street, his landscaping looked the best. It was right then and there that Camille knew she was going to give SK some pussy.

"Can I get you something to drink?" SK asked, leading Camille into the kitchen.

Camille hopped up on the island that sat in the middle of the kitchen. "I'm not gonna lie. I was thinking about you last night."

SK walked over to her with two bottles of water and passed one to her. "Oh, yeah? And what was you thinking about?"

"I was thinking that I want you to beat dis pussy up. You think you can handle that?" Camille asked before grabbing SK by the shirt and pulling him closer to her.

If SK weren't so dark skinned, she would have been able to see him blush. "Come wit' me," he told her as he attempted to take her hand.

Camille smiled seductively and wrapped her legs around his waist while shaking her head no. She reached down, grabbed the bottom of his T-shirt, and pulled it up and over his head. "Right here!" she insisted.

SK slid his hand under her dress and caressed her thighs until he hiked her dress up enough to pull off her panties. Camille did the rest, pulling the dress over her head. Her body was crazy, and SK's dick damn near cut through his pants. He went in for the kill, grabbing the back of her neck and pulling her to his mouth.

Heavy kissing and rubbing on her breasts led to Camille unfastening his belt and then yanking his pants down enough so that his dick was free. He climbed up onto the island, lay on top of her, and pushed his long, thick, stiff pole inside of her.

Camille's jaw dropped in shock as his dick filled her canal. It was bigger than what she expected.

"Take it like a big girl!" SK teased, pushing every inch of it into her.

After a few strokes, the pain had subsided and the pleasure had begun. SK didn't play any games with her either, lifting both of her legs up and over her shoulders while he continued pounding away.

Loud cries from Camille's open mouth sounded throughout the kitchen, and from the way SK handled her body, she could feel an orgasm coming on. "Hit it harder!" she moaned while caressing her breasts and nipples.

SK had no problem accommodating her, slamming his dick in and out of her violently.

Camille was loving it, too, so much so that it brought on that first orgasm she'd felt from the start. "Oooohhhh, shit!" she cried out, reaching around for anything to grab hold of.

Her thin, clear cum shot out of her box and onto SK's dick. For a minute he thought that she had pissed on him, but then he quickly realized that she was cumming. He himself wasn't ready to bust just yet. Now that she was nice and wet, he was about to take her for a ride she'd never been on before, and from the looks of how she was enjoying herself, she was ready to take it all.

Chapter 6

The rest of the weekend shot by fast, and before Dion knew it, she was walking through the front doors of the courthouse with her legal team behind her. She was in beast mode and wasn't about to play any games getting her husband home today.

"I'ma sit in the back," Sarita told Nasir, seeing that the courtroom was packed. She didn't know why so many people were there. The case seemed to be more serious than what she thought. Hassan's case was the second one on the docket, so it took a little while before they called his case number.

"Commonwealth of Pennsylvania vs. Darnell Johnson!" the bailiff called out.

At the same time, Hassan was being brought out from the back of the courtroom in handcuffs. The district attorney nodded at Detective White, who was standing in the back of the courtroom.

White stepped out into the hallway for a second and then came back in with Camille.

When Sarita saw her aunt walking down the center aisle, she damn near jumped out of her skin. Camille didn't see Sarita sitting in the back of the courtroom, and she wanted to keep it that way, so she scooted all the way into the corner, then sank down low in her seat. "What da fuck is going on?" she mumbled to herself, confused as to why Camille was there.

The people in the courtroom looked on as the DA began to speak. "Your Honor, the Commonwealth has filed charges against Darnell Johnson on conspiracy to commit second-degree murder and first-degree sexual assault for the rape of Camille Scott."

Dion cut right in. "Your Honor, this case is well over fifteen years old."

"Yes, but the statute of limitations doesn't go away when a homicide is involved," the DA corrected her.

"And what new evidence does the Commonwealth have this time around that they didn't have before?" the judge asked the DA.

"Your Honor, aside from the legally seized DNA taken from Mr. Johnson, we also have one of the victims who was there during the crime back in September of 1990."

The judge took his glasses off, wiped the corners of his eyes, then waved for the DA to bring her witness to the stand. This was like déjà vu to Camille, who remembered this entire process like it was yesterday.

"Ms. Scott, would you please tell the court what happened to you on the night of September 19, 1990?" the DA began.

Camille sat there for a moment trying to get her thoughts together. Sarita, on the other hand, sat in the back of the courtroom, stunned and confused.

"I went with my sister and my best friend to Mr. Johnson's house one evening, and while we were there, all of us were drugged and raped. My best friend was killed, and me and my sister lived," Camille explained.

"And as a result of you being raped, what happened to you physically?"

Camille didn't want to answer the question. It was hard enough being there in the first place.

The DA didn't let up though. "Ms. Scott, please tell the court what happened to you as a result of you being raped."

Camille was silent yet again. She looked around the courtroom to see who was there. If Sarita weren't so sunk down in her seat, she would have seen her, and Camille definitely wouldn't have spoken as freely as she was about to. "I got pregnant," she said in a low voice.

"Can you speak up, Ms. Scott?" the judge asked.

"I got pregnant!" she yelled out.

"And did you have the baby?" the DA pressed.

Irritated, Camille answered, "Yeah! Now can we move on? I'm starting to get pissed off!"

"I'm sorry, Ms. Scott. I know this is difficult for you. But do you see the man who raped you in the courtroom today?" the DA asked.

Darnell, who now went by the name Hassan, was lightweight and had dreadlocks back then. But even now Camille would never forget his face. This was the first time she'd laid eyes on Hassan since 1998, which was the year Judge Cook dismissed the charges against him in court. She looked into his eyes, and it seemed like the whole incident came back to her at once. It was overwhelming, but she still managed to point to Hassan.

"Let the record show that Camille Scott has identified Darnell Johnson," the DA announced. "And is the man who killed your best friend in the courtroom today?" he asked.

As badly as Camille wanted to, she didn't want to lie about the murderer. "No, he's not in the courtroom. But Darnell let it happen!" she blurted out.

Sarita knew the name Darnell Johnson, of course, from the story her grandmother told her. Putting it together, she could see why Isis and Camille were so nasty and bitter toward her, because she was the product of a rape. That was enough to drive anybody mad.

Sarita reached into her back pocket and pulled out the picture that she and Shay had printed out from the computer. She looked at it and then to Hassan. She looked at the picture again and then back at him. It was definitely him. Her mouth began to water, indicating that she was about to throw up. She knew she wasn't going to make it to the bathroom, so she opened up her Coach bag and barfed inside. She really couldn't believe what she had heard, and the weight of it all was too much to handle. She couldn't sit there for another moment, and as soon as she got herself together, she quietly got up and left the courtroom.

SK pulled into Busti Projects by himself with only a compact .45 and the hunger to take over the city. Busti Projects was Hassan's main source of income, and if SK wanted to be successful in his takeover, he needed to start here.

"Muthafucka got some nuts," Chuck commented when SK got out of his truck.

"Cool out, homie. I'm not here for all dat," SK said, walking up to Chuck.

"I ain't ya mafuckin' homie!" Chuck checked while mean mugging SK.

"You right, but dig dis, young blood. I hear ya boss is in some hot water, and even though we ain't the best of friends, I'm tryin'a extend my hand," he said, leaning up against Chuck's car.

"And how da fuck are you supposed to do that? Look around, nigga. Do it look like I need a hand?" Chuck snapped.

SK was getting a little tired of Chuck's aggression and lack of respect, but at the same time he didn't want to blow the spot up and defeat the purpose of why he was there. "Just hear me out, cuz, and if you don't like what I say, I'll get out of ya hair," SK continued. "I know y'all gotta be paying like seventy grand a key for heroin, and nine times out of ten, it's probably gonna be stepped on once or twice before y'all get it. But I can give it to you for sixty grand a pop just as long as you buy ten or better. Shit's so raw you can cut it four times and it'll still be the best shit around."

Chuck pulled a cigarette from his pack and put it up to his mouth. He stood there thinking about it, debating whether he should play ball. The product that Chuck had was getting low, and missing the shipment from Hassan's supplier last week was really making him consider the move. Chuck never got a chance to tell Hassan about the missed shipment, and he knew that Hassan was going to be mad about that, especially since the connect wasn't going to be back for a few months. SK wasn't the best option, but he might be Chuck's only choice to make things right.

"So now what?" Hassan looked over and asked Dion after the judge made his ruling on the bail issue.

Being that Hassan had posted bail on this case before and had made every court hearing, the judge granted him the same bail as before, but this time he made him stay on house arrest until the trial was over. He still had to put up some property, which had to be the equivalent of $1 million, but that was nothing.

"So now I have to go through the whole paperwork process again!" Dion said with an attitude.

Hassan could see that something was bothering her and had an idea of what it was. "Come downstairs and see me before you leave the courthouse," he told her right before the sheriff walked over to the table.

Dion grabbed her briefcase, got up, and walked out of the courtroom without saying anything. She didn't even look at Hassan, and for the entire walk back down to the holding cell, Hassan didn't think she was going to come see him. But eventually she did, and he could see that she was upset.

"You mean to tell me that after all these years, you still don't believe me?" he asked, trying to get Dion to look at him. "I'll tell you again, just like I told you back then. I did not rape that girl!"

"But why is she still so certain of it? I mean, I believe you, but damn, Hassan!" Dion replied, shaking her head in frustration.

Dion did believe him for the most part, but just seeing Camille back on the stand brought back so many memories. Dion was the one who represented Hassan back then, and the things she had to go through to get the charges thrown out were exhausting. So many of her morals as a woman were compromised, and she would hate to have to go through that again.

"Dion, you know I love you, right?"

"And I love you too. That's why I'm still here," she said as she gathered her things. "I have to start the paperwork so you can come home. We'll have more than enough time to talk when you get there," she concluded.

Her attitude was a little better before she left, but Hassan knew that this wasn't going to be the end of it. The good part about it was that he still had her on his side, and if he had any chance of beating this case and ducking a life sentence, he was going to need her. She wasn't just good at what she did, she was great, and if there was anybody who could get him a verdict of not guilty, it would be Dion.

"Sarita! Sarita!" Nasir yelled out as he ran down the street after her. He was hoping to catch her before she got on the bus. Luckily he did, but she wasn't in the mood to talk. "Damn, girl! Hold up for a second!" he said, grabbing hold of her arm.

Sarita turned around and almost threw up again at the thought of her possibly having sex with her own brother.

"Listen, this shit is all new to me too. I swear, I didn't know that he was being accused of—"

"Ya dad is a fuckin' creep!" Sarita snapped, cutting him off.

Nasir couldn't deny how messed up Camille's allegations were. "But why are you staring at me like that? You think I'm capable of doing some shit like that?" he questioned.

It crossed her mind for a moment, but the main reason she was staring at him was to see if there was any resemblance of herself in him, being that they might have the same father.

"What?" Nasir asked. He was becoming a little uncomfortable with her staring.

"Nothing," Sarita replied. "I have to catch this bus," she said as the bus pulled up to the stop.

Nasir didn't want her to leave, not like this anyway. He wanted to separate himself from Hassan's situation, even if that meant disclosing some of the family secrets. "He's not really my dad," he said in a final attempt to keep her from getting on the bus.

Sarita turned around and looked at him. "What did you say?" she asked, looking him in his eyes.

"I said that's not my real dad. He's not my biological dad, anyway. My real dad is dead."

"Stop fuckin' lying to me, Nasir! That is ya dad!" she snapped. She wanted that to be the truth more than anything. Considering all that happened today, she was skeptical of believing anything anybody in that family said.

"Just come with me. I'll explain everything to you," Nasir said, holding his hand out. "Please," he said, seeing Sarita hesitate.

The bus driver had closed the doors and pulled off, not wanting to wait any longer for her. That, along with the fact that she wanted to know the truth, compelled her to take his hand and go with him.

SK didn't get halfway down I-95 before his cell began vibrating in the center console. He smiled when he saw Chuck's number pop up on the screen. The deal he offered Chuck was too much like right, and anybody who was in the dope game couldn't pass up a deal like this. "Yo, what it do, bro?" SK answered as he maneuvered through the traffic.

"Text me a time and a location, and I'll be there to see you," Chuck responded, and then hung up the phone before SK could say anything. He wanted to keep his conversation short and sweet over the phone.

SK did lie about one thing though, and that was that he wasn't in fact the person who had the heroin for sale. He only dealt with cocaine, but he had a supplier who would pretty much give him anything he wanted for the low, especially heroin. It was nothing for him to get a key of heroin for fifty grand, and if he was buying more, the price would go down as well. Not only would he be able to step on the product to make some extra money, but he was also going to have his hands in the west side of Philly where the real money was being made. In the back of his mind, he knew that once he was in, he was going to take over completely. And whoever had a problem with it was going to be dealt with accordingly.

"My real dad was in the streets, knee-deep in the game, when my mom got pregnant with me. And from what I hear, he had the city on lockdown," Nasir began as he drove. "Everybody in the city had love for him. He had connections with the cartel and made sure everybody was making money. The Feds hated him because they knew he was the number one guy but couldn't be touched. His hands never touched any of the drugs, and nobody in the city was willing to snitch on him.

"One night while my dad was on his way to pick up my mom, an unmarked police car pulled my dad over. I was in my car seat. The detective walked up to the driver side of the car and fired two shots into my dad's chest. He later died at the hospital, but not before telling my mom what had happened. The cop lied and said that my dad pulled a gun on him and that was the reason why he shot him. Come to find out my dad didn't even have a gun in the car. Muthafuckin' police killed my dad!" Nasir explained while shaking his head.

Sarita sat there actually feeling sorry for him. Dion was the one who told Nasir the story after he got up in age, and there were also a few people who confirmed the story to Nasir, which made him believe it.

"Yeah, so a couple of years later when I was about two years old, she met da nigga Hassan, or whatever the nigga's name is," Nasir said. "I only called him my dad because he was the only adult male in my household for as long as I could remember."

After hearing the story, coupled with the fact that Nasir didn't look like Hassan, Sarita believed him. But to the contrary, she wasn't about to divulge her secret of who Hassan was to her. She didn't want to for a number of reasons, but the most important one was that she still planned on killing Hassan if and when he got out of jail. It would be tragic if Nasir—or anybody else for that matter—got in her way. This was the only remedy she could come up with after all the shit she'd been through. Not just that, but finding out that Camille was her mother and she was the product of a rape did something to her mentally. She wasn't in her right mind at all. It was depressing, and killing Hassan was the only thing that would make her feel just a little bit better about herself.

Mrs. Scott was startled when she heard a loud bang on the door, and when she walked out of the kitchen, she could see Sarita looking through the front window. "Girl, did you lose ya mind?" she asked when she opened the front door.

Sarita stormed past her, and it became obvious that something was wrong. "You know, Grandma, out of everybody in our family, I thought that you would be the one I could trust. I thought if there was anybody who cared or loved me, it was you." She could barely talk because she had a knot in her throat the size of a plum, and the tears began to flow from her eyes.

"Baby, I do love you," Mrs. Scott said, walking up to her. She tried to wipe the tears from Sarita's face but was met with a slapping of her hand. She gave Sarita one of those looks.

"Well, if you love me so much, then tell me who my real mother is, Grandma!"

It caught Mrs. Scott off guard to the point where she froze.

"Please don't lie to me. I will walk out this door, and you will never see me again!" Sarita warned.

Mrs. Scott took one look in Sarita's eyes and could see the hurt, pain, anger, and confusion. The secrets this family had were too much to bear for anybody, and it was at this point Mrs. Scott couldn't hold it in any longer. She couldn't be the gatekeeper of lies anymore, and if it was the truth Sarita was seeking, then that was what she was going to get. "Camille is your biological mother," she began. The weight of that statement alone was heavy enough to force her to take a seat on the couch.

"Why? Why lie to me all these years?" Sarita snapped. She paced back and forth in the living room letting off some steam, and her grandmother continued.

"After Camille was raped, she became pregnant with you. Nicole and I convinced her not to abort you. When you were born, Camille couldn't stand to look at you. She said you looked just like him." Mrs. Scott's eyes began to fill with tears as she continued the story. "So one night when Camille was supposed to be giving you a bath . . ." She broke down and had to take a moment to get herself together before continuing. "You were in the bathtub drowning while Camille stood by the sink and just watched."

Sarita stopped pacing and looked at her grandmother in shock.

Mrs. Scott wanted to stop, but she pushed through. "So after that, Nicole convinced Camille to let her adopt you and raise you as her own child. Nicole's boyfriend at the time was Wendell Powell. They called him—"

"Wink," Sarita finished.

"He changed your last name to his and raised you and Channel like sisters, that is up until Nicole passed away, and then he went to prison. Camille took legal guardianship of you two when you were about seven. She raised Channel as her daughter and you as her niece."

"That's why Isis calls her Mom!" Sarita cut in. "Why didn't you do something? Why didn't you take me in and raise me?" Sarita started crying again, thinking about how all of her life's struggles would have been prevented if her grandmother had stepped in.

"I tried, baby. You have to believe me when I tell you I tried. But that Camille can be an evil person, and I'm too old to be fighting with that girl. So I kept my distance for a long time, and then I slowly incorporated myself back into you girls' lives. It was a struggle, but Camille wasn't financially capable of taking care of two kids by herself, and that's when I stepped in."

By the end of the story, Sarita's anger toward her grandmother had subsided. Despite everything that had happened, Mrs. Scott played a pivotal role in her life growing up, and because of that alone she was grateful for her grandmother. She loved her grandmother, and though she was confused and upset right now, she could never hold anything against her.

Camille, on the other hand, was now the target of Sarita's anger, and there would come a time when they'd have this conversation face-to-face with nobody to get in between.

Chapter 7

Shay walked into the bedroom and said, "Girl, if you don't get ya ass up out of that bed, I'ma throw a bucket of water on you! We only have prom once, so we gotta do it big," she said, pulling the curtains back to let the sunlight into the room.

Sarita darted under the covers like she was a vampire who didn't want to be burned by the sun. "I'm not going!" she yelled from under the blanket. The last time she'd spoken to Nasir was the day of Hassan's court date. Not wanting to be in the same house as Hassan when he got home from jail, she sought refuge in Shay's guest room. She didn't even know if Nasir still wanted to go.

Shay wasn't trying to hear any of it though. She snatched the blanket off Sarita, exposing her to the light. "We been planning this day since we was in elementary school, and you will not be selfish and ruin it for us," she said, and pulled her phone from her pants pocket.

Sarita sat up in the bed with a curious look on her face, wondering who Shay was texting. Moments later, Sarita's phone on the nightstand began to vibrate. She rolled her eyes at Shay when she saw that it was Nasir calling her.

"Damn! I was hoping you answered my call," Nasir spoke. "How are you, and where have you been?" he asked out of concern.

"I'm doing okay. I just needed some time to think." Sarita had to admit that she did miss him a lot. Things just weren't the same after she found out who Hassan really was.

"So look, I know we haven't spoken all week, but I wanted to know if you still want to go to the prom. I really wanna go, but I'm not going if I can't have you by my side," Nasir said.

Sarita looked over at her dress hanging up in Shay's closet. She really didn't feel like going, but hearing Nasir's voice changed her mind. She hadn't been out of the house all week, and some fresh air was needed. Plus, Shay was right when she said that prom happened once in a lifetime. "I'll meet you at ya house around five," Sarita said with a smile on her face.

As soon as Sarita ended the call with Nasir, Shay danced her way toward the bathroom. "Now get ya ass up!"

Dion walked out onto the back patio where Chuck and Hassan were discussing some business. She didn't stay long and only wanted to let Hassan know that the probation officer was going to be stopping by today. After relaying that to him, she went back into the house.

"So where da fuck am I supposed to get product from?" Hassan snapped. Chuck had told him about missing the shipment date with Alonzo, the supplier, and Hassan was pissed about that. "I sat there and asked you if you could handle that shit."

"I know, bro. I fucked up, but I found somebody else. Da muthafucka got some bomb shit, too," Chuck explained, and pulled out an ounce of the heroin that he had bought from SK. After testing it out, he bought one kilo just to see how many times he could step on it before it started to lose its potency. He had turned one kilo into two, and it was still the best product in the city.

"So who da fuck is it?" Hassan asked, wanting to know who in Philly had product for sale besides him and his connect.

Chuck wasn't about to tell Hassan that it was SK, at least not right now. Though Hassan didn't think that SK was the one who tried to kill him, tensions were still running high between the two men, and anything could set either one of them off. For that reason alone, Chuck lied and said that the product came from somebody out of town. He made up a fake name and history of where he knew the supplier from. He even lied about the prices, telling Hassan that a kilo was going for $67,000 a pop.

Hassan sat there and thought about it. His original supplier wasn't going to be back in town for months, and he was down to his last kilo, which wouldn't last through the week. "A'ight, if the dope is what you say it is, then let's do it. I only want ten keys of that shit right now. Alonzo should be back in the city by the time we're done with that. And if he's not back by then, we'll buy just enough from ya connect until my man does get back. You got me?" Hassan asked with a stern look on his face.

Chuck knew that he was treading on thin ice. "No doubt, my nigga," he said before standing up to get ready to leave.

Hassan had to warn him one more time just in case Chuck didn't understand the magnitude of what he was saying. "Don't fuck dis up. Don't make me lose confidence in you being able to run shit while I'm out of commission."

Chuck gave him dap and assured him that he could be depended on and would get the job done.

"When it comes to this dope shit, it's a whole other ball game," SK explained as he and Bishop sat at the kitchen table. Aside from them, Camille was the only other person there and was cooking the guys something to eat.

"Now Hassan got his foot on the west side, but his man said that we can post up here and here," SK explained, pointing to Fifty-second and Fifty-fifth Streets on the map of the city. "Shit gets crazy around these parts, so we gotta find a nigga crazy enough to transport the product over to our guys without getting killed. You got stickup boys and the police waiting for new niggas to show up in the hood," he continued.

West Philly had become the most dangerous section of the city, and even though Chuck gave him the okay to do his thing in those two areas, Chuck couldn't make it official, so SK was still taking a big risk. That meant SK and his boys were going to have to get in where they fit in all on their own.

"I'll do it," Camille volunteered. She walked over and put SK's plate on the table in front of him. She listened to the whole conversation and knew that her skin complexion could help out in what they were trying to accomplish. It was also a bonus that she used to live in West Philly and knew the area well.

"If you got somebody for me to deliver the product to, then I'll do it."

"Damn, that's perfect! Nobody's gonna even think to mess wit' you. And it will save us money not paying niggas to transport."

Camille quickly checked him on that. "Slow down, playboy! I'm not moving product for free," she intervened.

SK smiled, liking her hustle mentality.

"I'll need fifteen hundred for every delivery I make out there. I don't care if it's an ounce or a brick. And I need mine up front, too."

Bishop looked at SK, who gave a nod of approval.

The price for her services was worth it, and SK was even more impressed that she didn't let her personal feelings toward him get in the way of her making money. That was some G shit, and at the same time it was a turn-on. Now he was going to see how far she was really willing to go. "Now, let's get dis muthafuckin' money!" he concluded.

"I'll get it," Dion said after hearing the doorbell ring. When she opened the door, Sarita was standing there looking amazing in her dress. "Oh, my God, you look nice! Come in. Nasir will be down in a minute," Dion told her. She then went upstairs to get him.

"Damn, li'l mama! You doing ya damn thing!" Hassan said while coming out of the kitchen with a sandwich in his hand. "Um, um, um! Y'all better keep it PG tonight!" he added, seeing how Sarita filled out her dress. He walked all the way up to her and stood a mere couple of feet away with a perverted look in his eyes.

"I see you made it home," Sarita said.

"Yeah. They can't keep a good nigga down. I saw you in the back of the courtroom the other day. Thanks for coming out."

"I was there for your son, not you," Sarita said with an attitude. It took everything in her not to flip out on him.

Hassan could sense a little bit of hostility, and he knew that it probably came from what she heard in the courtroom. The last tag Hassan wanted on his record was him being a rapist. "Don't believe everything you hear. I—"

"Hassan, leave that girl alone!" Dion yelled from the top of the stairs.

At the same time, Nasir was coming down the stairs with a mean mug on his face. Their relationship had been strained ever since Hassan had come home. "Come on, let's get out of here," he said to Sarita as he quickly tried to usher her out the door.

"What? We can't get no pictures?" Hassan reached for his phone.

"Yeah, just a couple," Dion chimed in.

Nasir shot the idea down. "Nah, we good with the flicks," he said. He took Sarita by the hand and headed toward Dion's S550.

Hassan felt some type of way and was going to say something, but Dion pulled him back into the house before he could. She knew her son better than anybody and knew that it was going to take some time along with a serious conversation in order for him to shake the rape allegations Hassan had on him.

Camille looked back at SK as he pounded her from behind. Her ass could be heard clapping up against his pelvis, and the faster he stroked, she knew that he was about to bust. She reached back with one hand and spread her ass cheeks apart so he could go deeper. She too felt an orgasm coming, which would be her third this session. She grabbed the headboard with one hand, grabbed her breast with the other, and threw her ass back at him.

Faster, deeper, and harder, SK slammed his dick inside of her as he was reaching his point. He came to the conclusion that pulling out wasn't an option. His thick, creamy cum squirted inside of Camille, which in return made her cum as well. He could see both his and her fluids all over his dick as he continued to stroke. This was the first time he'd fucked Camille without a condom, and being honest with himself, this was the best pussy he'd ever had, and cumming inside of her was his way of letting her know.

Flopping down on the bed, Camille asked, "Damn, bae! What are you trying to do to me?"

SK flopped down right next to her and wrapped his arms around her, pulling her close. "I'm making you mine. You got a problem wit' that?" he asked, playfully biting her on the shoulder.

"So what are you saying? You want me to be ya girl or something?"

It sounded crazy because he had only known Camille for a couple of weeks, but there was something about her that made him feel a certain type of way. She was gorgeous and book and street smart, she had A1 pussy, not to mention the fact that she could cook her ass off. "Yeah. I wanna make you my girl," he admitted before closing his eyes.

Camille could do nothing but smile, thinking how she was all for it. "I'm yours now, SK. And trust and believe, you won't be getting rid of me no time soon."

***

"Look at this dumbass nigga sitting out here selling this shit like its legal," Nasir said to Sarita as they pulled up to the projects.

Chuck was standing on a bench watching as his workers served every car that pulled up. They were selling quarters, halves, and ounces of heroin. This was the only time you would find Chuck out, while the drug traffic was this heavy. Any other time, he'd be far away from the hand-to-hand transactions.

"Damn! Wassup, li'l man? I see ya moms let you push the big boy toy tonight," Chuck said when Nasir rolled down his window. "Congratulations, too. I'm not gonna be in the city for ya graduation, but here," he said, and pulled out a wad of money. He didn't even count it as he peeled off half of it and gave it to him.

"Thanks, Unc. By the way, I was wondering what you had planned for the rest of the night," Nasir asked, hoping that Chuck would catch his look.

Chuck caught on instantly and looked from Nasir to Sarita. "I'm not doing too much of nothing," he answered, looking over the hood of the car at all the traffic that was coming through the projects. He reached into his pocket and grabbed the keys to his condo and passed them to Nasir. "Enjoy ya night, nephew. Now get out of here so I can get back to work." He tapped the roof of the car.

As they were pulling off, Sarita couldn't help but notice the tattoo of a "Jason" mask on Chuck's forearm. Immediately she thought about Camille's testimony and how she identified the second man in the house when she was raped. He wasn't the one who raped Camille, but he had something to do with it, and that was more than enough for Sarita to now have Chuck on her radar as well as Hassan. It was a place he really didn't want to be—or where anybody wanted to be for that matter.

Camille woke up after feeling SK standing behind her. When she looked up, he was getting dressed, trying not to wake her. "Where you goin'?" she whined. She didn't want him to leave.

As bad as SK didn't want to leave, he had to. "I gotta go make a move, but I'll be back in a couple of hours." He walked over to the bed and took a seat. Camille was there naked, making it hard for him to leave.

"Can I roll wit' you?" she asked.

Chuck had called and said he needed to holla at him, so more than likely he was about to put in an order for some dope. The possibility of danger was slim to none. "You really wanna ride?" he asked.

Camille jumped up and darted into the bathroom like a little girl. She took a quick shower and got dressed in record time. SK was already downstairs waiting for her.

On her way out of the room, she looked over and saw that he had left his Glock .40 on the nightstand. She quickly grabbed it and headed downstairs.

SK smiled when he saw the gun in her hand.

"Like American Express!" Camille said, handing him the gun.

"'Never leave home without it!'" SK said, completing the tagline. He lifted his shirt up to show the compact .45 on his hip. He was already strapped, but that didn't stop Camille from tucking the gun into her Hermès bag. That was just one of the reasons he was feeling Camille the way that he did. She was a stone-cold rida.

***

Nasir and Sarita stumbled through the front door of Chuck's condo. They both were a little tipsy from the night's events. The prom was a smash hit, and even though the dazzling couple wasn't crowned prom king and queen, everybody there treated them as though they were.

"Wow! This place is nice!" Sarita said, looking around the lightly furnished condo. It didn't look like anybody was occupying the place. That was because Chuck hardly ever stayed there.

"Oh, shit!" she gasped as she looked out at the city. The panoramic view of the city was breathtaking. She'd never seen Philly from this far up before.

"I gotta use the bathroom," she said, tossing her bag on the couch. She headed down the hallway while Nasir looked for some liquor.

The first door she opened wasn't a bathroom, but what she saw inside took her by surprise. "Oh, shit!" she mumbled, looking at piles of money all over the room. There was money on the bed, money on the dresser, and some falling out of several sneaker boxes by the bed. She had never seen that much money at one time.

"Sarita, where you at?" Nasir yelled from the living room.

Snapping out of it, Sarita took one last look at the money, then quickly closed the door. "I'll be right there!" she yelled back while walking a little bit farther down the hallway. After using the bathroom and giving herself a whore's bath in the sink, she headed back out into the living room, where Nasir was looking out the window at the city.

"Damn! We graduate in a couple of weeks," Nasir said as Sarita walked up behind him.

She wrapped her arms around his waist and placed her head up against his back. "I know. Things are moving much too fast," she said.

Nasir turned around, and without saying another word, he leaned in and kissed her. The passion escalated in a matter of seconds. Sarita moaned lightly as their lips locked on one another's. She began shedding his clothes, starting with his blazer. She damn near ripped his shirt off.

Nasir lifted her up and took her outside onto the balcony, where the night air felt refreshing. The city lights below them shined bright enough so they could see each other. He pressed her back up against the glass window, and their passion was ignited again.

Chapter 8

The rain was coming down like cats and dogs, but Hassan couldn't care less with the .357 Sig in his hand. He followed Sarita, who managed to crawl out into the parking lot. The bullet in her knee and another in her hip prevented her from running. The water dripped off the barrel of the gun as he raised it to Sarita's head.

The fear of God was in her eyes. She couldn't find the words to stop this execution. "Please! Please don't kill me!" was all she could think of. It wasn't enough by a longshot.

Hassan clutched the gun tighter and closed the distance between them until they were only about a foot or so apart. His heart was racing, and tears began to fill his eyes. Before he allowed his heart to change or his feelings to get the best of him, he pulled the trigger.

Pop!

The .357 slug knocked a chunk of meat out of her head as it entered, ripped through, and then exited her skull. He fired again to make sure there was no coming back.

The rainfall got stronger, washing away the blood from Sarita's head. Any guilt or hurt he felt about killing his own daughter had washed away with the water.

As he stood there looking over the body, Camille came from out of nowhere, raised the gun to the side of Nasir's head, and pulled the trigger.

Pop!

"Sarita! Sarita!" Shay called out, waking Sarita from her sleep.

Sarita damn near jumped out of her skin from the nightmare she'd just had. It felt all too real, and she could even taste the gunpowder from when Hassan blew her head off.

"Are you good?" Shay asked, seeing the pale look on Sarita's face.

Sarita cupped both her hands over her face, then flopped back down on the bed. Hassan killing her in her dream only enraged her to the point where today was going to be the beginning of Hassan's end. "Is Mason here?" she asked Shay.

"Yeah, why?" Shay asked with a concerned look on her face.

Sarita got dressed in a New York minute and was explaining her thoughts as she was doing so. "Do you plan on going to college, Shay?"

The question took Shay by surprise. "Of course I wanna go to college. But what in the hell does that have to do with anything?"

Sarita grabbed Shay by the arm and pulled her along. When they got downstairs, Mason was sitting in the living room playing *Call of Duty.* Sarita walked in and stood in front of the TV, blocking his view.

"Watch out!" he yelled, trying to peep around her.

Sarita then yanked the plug out of the socket.

"What da fuck!" Mason protested.

"Yeah, I know. She's tripping out right now," Shay intervened.

"Both of y'all shut up," Sarita began. "Now what if I told y'all that I can make us all rich? I mean, with more money than you'll even make in a lifetime? We can get out of the hood, go to college, and live comfortably for the rest of our lives."

"What are you talking about?" Shay asked, wondering where all this was coming from.

Sarita walked over and took a seat next to Shay on the couch. "Darnell," Sarita said with a straight look on her face.

Shay immediately jumped up from the couch. "No, no, no! I'm not gonna help you kill ya dad," she said.

Mason had a confused look on his face.

"He is not my dad!" Sarita shot back, jumping up from the couch. "I'm not gonna kill him. I'm just gonna take him for everything he has," she lied. She definitely was going to kill Hassan, but she just didn't want Shay to know that right now. "You don't think he deserves this after all that I been through?" Sarita asked, running her guilt trip on Shay.

"You gon' get us killed messin' around wit' that man's money."

"No, I'm not. I can find out anything I want about him," Sarita assured her. "Everything we take, we'll split right down the middle."

Mason was still sitting there looking confused. He looked back and forth from Sarita to Shay as they talked. All he knew so far was that there was money involved.

"I swear won't nobody get hurt. I need you with me on this one, Shay."

Shay sat there thinking about it, and even if she didn't want to, she was in no position to deny her bestie any aid and assistance. They'd been through everything together, and the buck wasn't about to stop here. "I swear, bitch, you better not get me killed!" she said, poking Sarita in her chest.

They shared a hug, then turned around to look at Mason, who still had a confused look on his face.

"Whatever y'all crazy chicks got goin' on, I'm in," Mason said. "I just got one request though."

"What?" both Shay and Sarita asked in unison.

"Can one of y'all please plug the game back up?"

Camille stopped at the light and began to check herself in the mirror. She looked pretty cool for a female who had 500 bundles of heroin in her possession. In street value, that was $75,000 worth of product, hopefully to be sold in a few days on the west side.

SK and Bishop had their hands in the west side, particularly down at the bottom. The product that he had in the Busti Projects had dopefiends overdosing. The fiends expected the dope to be cut like they were used to, but instead it was three times stronger. When word of that got around, other dopefiends in the neighborhood and surrounding neighborhoods wanted to see what it was hitting for.

Bishop's boy went from doing one bundle a shift to doing thirty bundles a shift, all in a matter of a few days. In a week's time, this was Camille's second drop-off to SK's boys, and by the looks of things, she'd be making another one before the weekend was over.

"Mom, have you heard from Sarita?" Isis asked as she looked out the passenger-side window at the passing cars.

"No, she hasn't contacted me. My mom said that she's okay though."

"I hope she's okay. I know we got into a fight and all, but I kinda miss her," Isis said.

"Aw, look at you, getting all soft on me," Camille teased. She didn't want to show Isis her softer side, but she too was a little concerned about Sarita. Having a daughter but not being in her life as a mother played on Camille's thoughts at night. She knew that she was wrong for the way she treated Sarita, but pride, anger, and selfishness clouded her motherly instinct. "You two have a court date coming up soon, so we should see her there. Maybe we can sit down and iron things out," Camille said, reaching over and tapping Isis on the arm.

Right now wasn't the time to be getting sentimental. Camille had a trunk full of heroin that she needed to get to the west side in one piece. That was what she felt she needed to focus on right now, not Sarita.

Hassan opened the front door only to see Sarita standing there. He was expecting someone else. "You know, Nasir isn't here. His mom took him down to North Carolina to take a tour of the college," he told her.

"I know he's not here. I actually came to see you. I need to speak to you about something."

"Ah, this should be interesting," Hassan said, stepping to the side to let Sarita in. Before closing the door, he took a peek outside to make sure that she had come alone, which she had.

"Damn!" he mumbled to himself, closing the door. His perverted eyes couldn't help looking at Sarita's firm, round ass walking into the dining area. For a moment he thought he was about to luck out and get a shot of pussy.

"So what can I do for you?" he asked, leaning up against the partition.

Sarita took a seat at the dining table. "It's no secret what you do out here in the streets. I was hoping that you could find something for me to do so I can make some money. College is right around the corner."

Hassan smiled, walked over, and took a seat at the table with her. "So what kind of work are you looking for?" he asked in a perverted way while looking down at Sarita's thick thighs.

His gaze sent chills all over Sarita's body in the worst way. If she'd had a gun on her, she probably would have shot him in the face. "No, not like that," she corrected him. "I used to sell weed at school. Plus, I know my way around the hood."

Hassan sat back in his chair while thinking about a position she could play on his team. He really didn't have a lot of females working for him, and the few he did have were straight-up hood rats. Sarita was a little too cute and smart to be around them. But he did want to come up with something good in hopes that he would impress her enough to get a shot of some young pussy.

"A'ight, a'ight, I got something for you. Now don't get it fucked up. I run my shit like a real company. I need eight hours a day, Monday through Friday. You'll get paid twenty-five hundred dollars every Saturday morning, plus a bonus if you do good. You'll be able to pay for college and anything else you need in no time," he told her.

"So when can I start?" Sarita asked.

Hassan looked at his watch and was reminded that one of his workers had called not too long ago and needed some help. "You can start right now," he told her.

That was the answer Sarita was hoping to hear. What she didn't expect was the conversation they were about to have.

"I didn't get a chance to holla at you about my situation," Hassan began. "My son is pissed at me, and I know he must think the worst of me," he said, getting up from the table and walking toward the kitchen. "What about you? I saw the way you looked at me that day."

"To each his own. Just as long as you don't try that goofy shit with me, or else you'll lose ya dick!" Sarita replied, following him into the kitchen.

Hassan turned around and looked into Sarita's eyes. "I didn't do what that chick said I did. She's a liar and I got proof. You'll see. Everybody will see in court," Hassan assured her.

Sarita wasn't trying to hear anything he was talking about. In her mind, he was already guilty and was going to be judged by her well before the trial date. But before that happened, she was going to be sure that he died with nothing.

Chapter 9

Mason and his boy walked through the front lobby of the Maple Tree Condominiums looking cool, calm, and relaxed. The night security guard didn't give them a second glance as they hopped onto the elevator.

"I hope dis muthafucka ain't home," Rando said, adjusting the 9 mm on his hip.

"It's Friday night at the start of the summer. Who in their right mind is gonna be in the house?" Mason replied.

"Well, if he is, then that's on him. It's lights out."

Mason knew that he had to check Rando before things got out of hand. Sarita specifically said that nobody was to get hurt, and Mason gave his word that he was going to avoid it at all costs. Rando was his boy though, and he wouldn't want to do a home invasion with any-body else. But at the same time, he knew that Rando was a shooter for real. He was like a black version of Billy the Kid. "Only if we got to turn this robbery into a homicide," Mason said, looking up at the camera in the top right cor-ner of the elevator.

When they got off the elevator, there were cameras at both ends of the hallway. When they walked up to Chuck's door, they stood there in silence for a moment to see if they could hear anybody inside the apartment. It was quiet.

Sarita had clipped the keys to Chuck's condo from Nasir and had gotten an extra set made, so there wasn't any need for a forced entry. Mason just walked right through the front door, and Rando pulled his gun out immediately, closing the door behind him. The black bandanas that were around their necks quickly went over their faces. They went straight to the room Sarita sent them to.

As they walked down the hallway, Rando realized that there was somebody in the back bedroom. He tapped Mason on the shoulder, who quickly noticed it too. Leaving wasn't an option, nor was running the risk of somebody coming out of that bedroom and catching them.

Mason gave Rando a stern look. "No gunplay!" he whispered, and then nodded for Rando to go and secure the room. Rando wasted no time kicking in the bedroom door.

Chuck had a pretty, thick black chick in bed and was hitting her from the back. He looked over and saw the masked gunman but continued fucking like they weren't even there. The female didn't stop either.

"So you just gon' come up in my shit like this?" Chuck asked through his heavy breathing. "You must not know who you fuckin' wit'," he said before turning his attention back to the female as her ass clapped.

"I don't give a fuck who you are. Just keep ya nut ass in the bed," Rando warned.

Chuck started pounding away even harder, making the girl moan louder. Rando stood there watching with his gun in his hand.

At this point, Mason was in the money room, cleaning it out. There was even more money than what Sarita had described. There was also a large amount of heroin sitting off to the side. Mason took everything. "Yo, we out!" he yelled as he exited the bedroom.

Rando wasn't leaving yet. He walked over to the bed where Chuck was still humping, and grabbed the chrome .45 off the nightstand.

Chuck watched him the entire time while smiling. "You know I'm gonna kill you, right?" Chuck said, and pulled out of the young female. "I'ma kill you and who-ever put you on to me." Then he squirted his nut all over the girl's ass.

Rando backed out of the room with the gun still pointed at Chuck. "Yeah, but it's not gonna be tonight!" he taunted, then turned around and made a break for it.

The only other gun Chuck had in the condo was an AR-15, and chasing Mason and Rando with it through the condominium was a guaranteed jail sentence. The Maple Tree Condos were full of white people who didn't mind calling the cops at the slightest bit of aggression. They would show up in court with bells on on any given day. For that reason alone, Chuck let Mason and Rando go without a fight.

Sarita pulled up to Hoop Street and parked at the far end of the block, as instructed by Hassan. The job that he had for her was simple. She had to pick up money from different spots all over the west and southwest sides. This was her fourth stop today, and she had two other spots to hit before she punched out. The good thing about this job was that she never had to touch any drugs. Hassan had another runner to deliver the product.

When Sarita got out of the car, she stuffed the baby .380 into her back pocket. The gun was also given to her by Hassan, and he had another model to go along with it. "If you get robbed, there better not be one bullet left in your gun afterward," was what he told everybody who worked for him.

"You gotta be Sarita," a tall, slim guy said, coming down the steps to meet Sarita.

"Yeah, wassup? Are you ready?" she asked, getting right down to business.

"No doubt. Come on," he said, leading her into the house.

Like all the other spots she went to, Sarita took a mental note of everything: how many people were in the house, and which room had the money in it. And without question, just about everybody in the house carried a gun.

"How much is in here?" Sarita asked when the guy came back into the room with a Coach bag.

He explained that there was $10,000, but Sarita poured it out onto the glass coffee table anyway. She wasn't about to leave without counting it. If it was short, Hassan would have a fit, so counting every dollar was what she did. It took a few minutes to count, but all of the money was there.

The guy who brought her the money was named Vick, and he was feeling the way she was moving. "Damn! That's a good look for you," he said, watching Sarita walk out of the house and to her car.

Sarita smiled but didn't let him see it. She was kinda feeling herself too, never thinking that she had this type of bad-girl behavior in her. She had to admit she liked it.

***

"Damn, my nigga! Shit must be nice!" SK said when Chuck got out of the car. "You keep coppin' like this, I'm gonna have to start coming down on the prices."

Camille, who was sitting on the steps between his legs, nudged him when he said that.

"Shit, I'ma have to take you up on the offer," Chuck said. "Let me holla at you for a minute."

SK got up and started walking with Chuck down the project walkway. "Holla at me."

Chuck was down and out. Mason and Rando caught him with his pants down, literally. He didn't know it until he checked his money room. They had left him with nothing—no money, no dope. Hassan was going to be looking for his money soon. "Yo, homie, I need ya help. I just took a major loss, and I need you to front me some work for about a week," Chuck said. "My word, I'll get you right and I'll pay full price."

"Shit, my nigga! How much work are you talking about?" SK shot back.

"All I need is a key. I'll make it do what it do from there."

SK let out a whistle. The regular price for a kilo was seventy-five grand when buying a single kilo. He could get about sixty grand from his connect. But the thing was that he would have to use his own money to do it, being that his connect never gave work out on consignment.

SK's brain went into overdrive, thinking about how he could capitalize on Chuck's misfortune. "If I do this for you, I'm gonna need a favor in return," he said as they continued walking along. "So look. Ya folks down the bottom are resisting the movement. They shot at one of my boys the other night and told him to get da fuck out of there. I can't make no money if dudes is going to resist," he explained. "I need you to take care of that ASAP."

The bottom boys normally dealt with Hassan directly, but since he was put on house arrest, Chuck was handling all the affairs on that side. His word alone would give SK the green light to do his thing without any interruptions, along with relocating SK's boys to a better corner. In Chuck's eyes, this was only going to be temporary. As soon as Hassan's connect got back in town, it was back to the north side for SK. "That's a done deal. By tomorrow, everything will be a go," he assured SK.

With that being said, SK stuck his hand out to seal the deal.

Chuck didn't know it, but he was shaking hands with the devil.

"Who's the girl?" Detective Hill asked his partner as they sat a few blocks away from Hassan's house.

Sarita had just pulled up and was getting out of the Range Rover. She grabbed her bag and walked right into the house, using her own key.

"I'm not sure, but I think that's the son's girlfriend," Detective Smith answered, squinting his eyes to see.

"And what's that she's putting into her bag?" Hill asked.

Ever since Hassan was placed on house arrest, Detective Hill was watching him. He was waiting for Hassan to do something stupid so he could get his house arrest revoked, ultimately throwing him back in jail. The chances of Hassan winning his trial while behind bars were slim. As long as he was free, he would be able to stop Camille and intimidate her to the point where she wouldn't testify, which was something Hill couldn't have on his watch.

"Whoa, whoa! Hold on! Wait a minute!" Hill said, looking down the street. "Do you know of anybody having a detail on Johnson?" he asked.

"No, I haven't heard. Why? You see something down there?"

"Yeah, I think so. About a block and a half away."

A black Crown Victoria was sitting with the engine running, and two individuals were inside. Just to be sure, Detective Hill pulled out from where they were, crossed the intersection, then pulled up next to the car. It took a few seconds, but the dark-tinted driver-side window rolled down. Inside were two black males. Detective Hill thought he had something, but before he could get out of his car, the driver of the Crown Victoria held up his FBI badge. The agent was a little pissed at Hill for blowing up his spot, and Hill could tell. The agent didn't say a word, but rather pulled out of his spot and took a hard right at the intersection.

"Did you get the plate number?" Hill asked Smith as he pulled off behind the Feds.

"I'm already running them," Smith responded.

Hill stayed behind them as the tags were being run just in case the two men were imposters. But in this case they weren't. The plate came back as government issued, which meant that they were official.

Detective Hill hooked the next right, abandoning the tail. He didn't want to draw any more unnecessary attention to the federal agents. Plus, it was a must that he pull over and converse with Smith about what just took place. "The FBI," Hill said, throwing the gearshift into park. "What in the hell are they investigating?" he asked with a curious look on his face.

"I don't know, but if the Feds are watching him, that means it can't be good at all," Smith replied.

Hassan's problems were bigger than the rape allegations, and both detectives were going to find out how deep things really were.

Sarita switched cars at least twice before she actually made it to Hassan's house. When she got out of the car, she took the .380 from the center console and put it in her bag. As she was walking toward the house, her phone began to ring. It was Shay, hopefully with some good news. "Yeah?" Sarita answered before she got to the front door.

"It's done," Shay said, looking over at the large pile of money sitting on the kitchen table.

"A'ight, I'll be there in a few," Sarita replied before hanging up. Before she put the key in the door, she took the .380 from her bag and made sure she had a bullet in the chamber. She didn't trust Hassan one bit, and if he ever got it in his mind that he was going to rape her, she was going to remove those thoughts with a hot lead bullet.

"How did you make out?" Hassan asked as soon as Sarita walked through the front door.

She brushed past him. "Everybody came through except for those bottom boys. They said fast money had slowed up. The one kid didn't want to go into detail with me, but he said that he was going to holla at you about it. He did give me five stacks," she explained. "All the rest of the money is in the Range."

"Yeah, it's always something with those dudes. I'll have Chuck go and find out what's going on," Hassan said while walking into the living room, where he had some money sitting out on the coffee table. "Here," he said, passing Sarita a thin wad of bills.

She took it and held it up with a curious look on her face. She'd only been working for a day.

"I told you, payday is on Saturday," he said, looking at his watch.

He was right, too. Sarita didn't have a problem with it, stuffing the money into her back pocket. "A'ight, I gotta get out of here. Thanks," she said and headed for the door.

Hassan walked behind her and was a little too close. For a second, she thought that he would be stupid enough to try his hand, so she grabbed the butt of her gun inside her bag. Thankfully, he was only rushing to open the front door for her.

"I'll call you Monday morning. And, Sarita, if you stick with me, I'll make you rich. Just stay true to Nasir. He really does love you. Oh, and don't mind me. I can be a bit of an asshole sometimes. I really don't mean any harm, and I definitely don't want to make you uncomfortable. We good?" Hassan asked, sticking out his fist for a bump.

Sarita didn't want to give it to him, but she did anyway. She didn't know where all this was coming from, but it was what it was, and she was going to continue to do what she needed to. Despite Nasir having a creep for a stepfather, she had a lot of love for Nasir and wasn't going to do anything to betray him . . . at least, not intentionally.

When Sarita got back to Shay's house, the money was still sitting on the kitchen counter. The two kilos of heroin were also sitting there, the reason being that Rando, Mason, and Shay wanted to show their loyalty, honesty, and trust. They weren't going to touch anything until she got there. They even had a small conversation and agreed to make her the head of their newfound organization.

"What da hell is that smell?" Sarita asked, covering her nose.

"That's whatever is in those packages," Shay replied as they walked into the kitchen. "Mason and Rando went to the store . . ." She didn't finish her sentence before Rando and Mason walked through the front door.

"There y'all go. Is everybody okay?" Sarita asked when they walked into the kitchen.

"Yeah, we're good. It was an in-and-out job," Rando said.

"Yeah, and the muthafucka was home," Mason interjected. "We caught da nigga wit' his pants down!" he chuckled.

"Damn, my bad! I didn't think that he was going to be home," Sarita said and grabbed a stack of the money off the table. She looked at the pile of cash and concluded that there was a lot more money than what she saw when she was there. She didn't know how much money there was, but she was sure that they were going to have a good summer.

Chapter 10

Hassan finally got a day pass per the judge's instructions in order for him to attend to his legal businesses. Though the pass was only for six hours, he was going to make do with it. He had to check up on a few key people in his organization. But the main person he wanted to see was Chuck, which he was unable to do thus far. He hadn't seen him since last Friday, nor was Chuck answering his phone.

"Look, baby, I got an hour left," Hassan complained to Dion, who wanted him to stop by her office before he went home. He looked at his watch while standing in front of the elevator in Chuck's building. "Baby, if I have time to stop by, I will," he concluded. He had other pressing matters to attend to.

When he got up to Chuck's floor, he could smell the strong stench of heroin. He immediately became concerned, hoping that the smell wasn't familiar to anyone else in the building. He used his keys to gain entry into the apartment, and that was when he blew a gasket.

Chuck and two other people were standing in the living room by the pool table. They were cutting up heroin. This was in total violation.

"What da fuck is going on, Chuck?" Hassan asked with obvious anger written across his face. "You must'a bumped ya muthafuckin' head! You lookin' to go to jail?" Hassan snapped.

"I know, bro. My bad. But let me holla at you," Chuck said, leading Hassan toward the bathroom. He didn't want any of his workers to see him get checked by Hassan.

Hassan pointed at one of the workers. "Open up da fuckin' balcony door so some air can get in here! I can smell that shit all the way down the hallway!" he demanded.

He knew that something must have gone wrong. Cutting and packaging the product where you lived was a no-no, and one of the most important rules he lived by. Chuck had understood that up until now. The one thing Hassan feared more than any nigga on the streets was the Feds. They played no games, and they had no picks when it came to locking somebody up. They didn't just put you in prison. They ruined families in the wake of their wrath. They were pure evil, and Hassan didn't want any part of it.

"Brah, I got hit last week," Chuck began to explain as he took a seat on the bed. "Two muthafuckas with masks on walked right through my front door."

Hassan put his hand up in order to stop Chuck from speaking any further. "What da fuck you mean you got hit? How much did they take?" he asked, trying his best to stay calm.

Chuck lowered his head, not wanting to tell Hassan this part.

"How much did they take?" Hassan yelled, showing how pissed he was.

"They took a little more than four hundred thousand, plus two kilos of dope," Chuck answered in a low voice.

Hassan was so mad that he turned his head and looked to the sky for a second. "You dumb muthafucka!" he snapped and smacked Chuck upside the head. "You had all that shit here? I should kill you!" he continued as he poked Chuck in the head with his finger.

"I'ma get the money back, bro!" Chuck yelled back as he tried to avoid Hassan's finger. "Just give me a couple of days."

"You damn right you're gonna get the money back! I don't care if you gotta bag dis shit up and sell it hand-to-hand by ya self! Get my fuckin' money!"

Hassan didn't even want to be in Chuck's presence anymore. Standing there any longer, he would have forgotten that Chuck was his baby brother. Had it been anybody else, they would have been dead by now. He flung the bedroom door open and stormed out of the room. On his way out of the condo, he ordered the two workers to bag the dope up and get it out of there.

Sarita walked into the courthouse looking business savvy. She had on a gray suit by Tom Ford, a white blouse, and a pair of Christian Louboutin metallic sandals on her feet. On her face was a pair of clear-lens glasses by Ray-Ban. Her entire outfit was in the price range of $2,500. Her long, curly black hair was draped over her shoulders, and the deep-cleansing facial she got yesterday made her skin look vibrant.

She walked right past Camille and Isis, who were standing to the side talking to the public defender. Sarita didn't speak, or even look their way for that matter.

"Do you have a lawyer here with you today?" the bailiff walked over and asked Sarita, who was sitting at the table by herself.

"Yes. She should be here any second now." Sarita didn't have just any lawyer with her. She had Maria Vargas, the second-best trial lawyer in the city. Her retainer fee was $500 an hour. You could tell that Maria Vargas was a big deal because she and the DA walked into the courtroom together. They appeared to be sharing a laugh or two in the process.

"This will only take a few minutes," Maria said, taking a seat next to Sarita.

"It looks like that guy likes you," Sarita whispered, nodding over to the DA, who had glanced over his shoulder to look at Maria.

Maria looked at Sarita and winked just before everyone's attention focused on the judge who entered the courtroom.

"Your Honor, the Commonwealth has agreed to drop the charges as long as the defendants undergo a one-week anger management class," the DA said.

Maria leaned over and whispered, "You can go down there today, sign in, stay for fifteen minutes, and that will be the end of it."

Sarita nodded in agreement, and once the judge confirmed from both Sarita and Isis that they would attend the class, the assault charges against them were dropped. It literally took a few minutes, just as Maria said.

This was the easiest five grand Maria had made. "The next time you call me, make sure you have something juicy for me, like a homicide or at least an attempted murder!" she joked as they headed out of the courtroom smiling. "Now if you don't mind, I have some important matters to deal with in courtroom 105," she said, leaving Sarita standing in the hallway.

As Sarita was about to get on the elevator, Camille and Isis were coming out of the courtroom.

"Sarita!" Camille yelled out, walking ahead of Isis in hopes that she could have a word with Sarita alone.

Sarita turned around.

Camille stood there for a second checking Sarita out. "You look older and more mature," she complimented her. "So how are you?"

Sarita nodded her head. "I'm doing well. How about yourself?"

Camille paused, not really wanting to get into what her life consisted of. "I'm good. But about you—I know ya graduation is this week. I was wondering if I could come, or am I still on ya shit list?" she joked.

Sarita wasn't smiling though. "You can do whatever you want, Camille."

"'Camille'? Are you still calling me that after all that you know about me?"

Sarita looked at her like she was crazy. "What's that supposed to mean?"

"Oh, you still don't get it, do you? You sat in court that whole time and you still don't get it? You might wanna have another conversation with ya grandmother about me."

"Yeah, I know who you think you might be to me, but trust, you haven't been a mother to me since the day I was born. What you need to do is be honest with Isis. She's the one suffering right now, thinking you're her mother," Sarita chuckled. "Get ya shit together, Camille! And don't bother coming to my graduation!"

Hassan didn't get a chance to stop by Dion's office that day, so he knew she was going to be pissed when she got home. Nasir wasn't home, so Hassan figured that he would do something romantic to get back on her good side.

When Dion walked through the door, candles scented like vanilla, chocolate, and strawberry were placed all over the living room where he planned on serenading his wife for the night.

"How was work?" Hassan asked, walking out of the kitchen with a bowl of warm fudge syrup.

Dion definitely was upset at Hassan for not coming by her office today, but her anger was slowly being peeled away by his romantic gestures. "Why didn't you come by the office today? Thomas really wanted to talk to you," she said, stepping out of her heels.

Thomas, Dion's boss, was concerned about some of the heat the law firm was getting over social media about the rape and how their firm was representing him. A number of women stood out in front of the office to boycott the firm, and although they didn't lose any clients behind the protest, people were starting to support the group. That wouldn't be good for business in the long run.

"Look, babe. I know what Thomas wants, but I can't do it." Hassan wrapped his arms around her waist.

The romantic gestures were beginning to be of no use. "But if this is something that could clear your name, then I think you should do it," Dion shot back, removing Hassan's arms from around her waist. "It sounds stupid that you wouldn't want to clear your name. It makes you look guilty."

The romantic night he had planned was going to shit. He could sense the doubt manifesting in Dion's heart. It was the same kind of doubt that he thought they worked through fifteen years ago. "Dion, I'm not doing it. We gotta find another way to clear my name," he said in a stern voice.

"What about me? What about my job and our family? Doesn't any of that mean anything to you?" Dion asked, following him into the dining room.

"Dion, you sound stupid right now. But you know what? I think I know why." Hassan stopped and faced her, staring her in the eyes. "You must think I really raped that bitch."

"You know, at first I didn't. I took your word for it, but now . . ."

Hassan's whole facial expression changed. He went from being irritated to being downright angry. He felt insulted and totally disrespected. "I told you I didn't rape that girl!" he said through clenched teeth. "If you don't believe me, then you can get ya shit and get da fuck out!" he snapped, bumping her as he walked away.

The only reason Dion didn't follow him was because she knew that it would only make things worse. In her mind, she felt she probably crossed the line, but she couldn't help the way she felt. It was Hassan who made her feel this way in the first place, and until he put forth what evidence he claimed he had to prove his innocence, their relationship would continue to deteriorate, or until Dion took him up on his offer and left.

"Ah, shit! There she goes!" Eli exclaimed when Sarita got out of the car on Federal Street.

Just about everybody who worked for Hassan knew Sarita and liked her. She had also gotten familiar with those who were worthy of conversation.

"Eli, tell me something good." Sarita walked up the stairs.

"Everything looks good. But you gotta tell ya boy that we need that product coming a little faster."

He let Sarita into the house, and the normal people were there when she looked around. The collection was the same as it was for every trip. She sat at the table and counted out fifteen grand. Doing it like this had become a routine.

"Damn, Sarita! When you gon' let me take you out?" Eli asked, flirting with her as he always did when she came around.

Sarita smiled. "The day you leave the streets alone and get a real nine-to-five!" she chuckled.

Eli sat there thinking about something slick to say back to her, but he was interrupted by someone yelling in the front room. "Oh, shit! They got guns!" one of the workers shouted as he fell into the dining room where Eli and Sarita were sitting.

Walking right in and standing over the worker was Mason. The mask he had covering his face along with the shotgun in his hand told them that this was a robbery. He had the shotgun pointed right at Eli's chest.

Eli had a .45 on his hip, but he didn't want to take the risk of pulling it out, fearing he wouldn't be able to get a shot off.

Sarita, playing her part, reached for the .380 in her back pocket and pulled it out.

Mason turned the gun on her quickly, cocking a shell into the chamber. "Put dat shit down 'fore I blow ya muthafuckin' head off!" he warned her.

Sarita complied.

"Bitch, bag da fuckin' money up!"

Again, Sarita complied.

Now that the gun was pointed at her, Eli took a chance and pulled the .45 from his waist. He almost got a shot off, but Mason spoiled his plan, releasing buckshot into the center of his chest. The blast knocked Eli five feet backward onto his ass.

Sarita was fixated for a moment, looking at the numerous pellets that had opened up Eli's chest. She came to when Mason cocked the shotgun and pointed it back at her.

The worker on the floor was scared to death. "Just take the money and go!" he told Mason.

Mason kept his foot on the worker's back, reached over, and grabbed the bag of money off the table. "And you better not move!" he told Sarita and the worker as he was backing out of the room. As soon as Mason got to the door, he turned around and made a break for it.

Sarita quickly picked her gun up off the floor and began shooting as she headed toward the door. The worker jumped up, grabbed Eli's gun off the floor, and headed for the door as well.

By the time he got there, Sarita was standing on the porch watching as Rando and Mason took off running into the night. They were gone in a matter of seconds.

The money wasn't the only thing they took. While Mason was inside robbing the house, Rando was outside robbing the runner while he was delivering the dope to the house. It was unexpected, but a two-for-one deal for sure.

***

Hassan walked into the bedroom to find Dion zipping up her overnight bag. "I'm checking into the Four Seasons for a couple of days. I need to clear my mind," she told him.

He didn't try to stop her, nor did he say a word to her. Instead, he grabbed his phone off the dresser and walked right back out of the room.

Chapter 11

Sarita rested her head on Nasir's bare chest as they lay in bed during the morning hours. The television was on, and CNN was rebroadcasting last night's presidential debate.

"I know you gon' vote for Barack, right?" Nasir asked before changing the channel.

"You already know I'm all for the black man running the country," Sarita said. She rolled on top of him and straddled him. "Nasir, you should run for president. You'll definitely get my vote, and I'll be the freakiest first lady who ever hit Washington." Sarita leaned in to kiss him.

"Damn, I'm gonna miss you!" she said, thinking about him leaving on Monday. He had to go back down to North Carolina to meet and greet some important people. She wanted to go with him but needed to stay and take care of her business. "How about I make you some breakfast?" Sarita offered.

"Normally my mom wouldn't appreciate you burning up her kitchen, but since she's not here, I can go for some scrambled eggs, burnt sausage, and some toast." Nasir smiled.

Sarita playfully punched him in his chest and then got up to put on her pajamas. Nasir got up too, heading straight for the shower.

When Sarita got downstairs, Hassan came out of nowhere, scaring the hell out of her. He looked up the steps to see if Nasir was behind her, and once he saw that he wasn't, he grabbed her by the arm. "Come wit' me," he said, pulling her into the kitchen. "What da fuck happened last night on Federal Street?" he asked.

"I wasn't in the house for two minutes before a guy walked through the front door with a shotgun in his hand."

"Why da fuck didn't you call me?" Hassan shot back.

"I called ya phone ten times last night. I got here and Nasir answered the door. You was asleep."

"Damn!" Hassan blurted out.

A set of tires coming to a screeching halt grabbed both his and Sarita's attention.

"What da fuck!" Hassan mumbled to himself while walking to the front of the house. He saw Chuck's car through the window, and when he opened the door, he got an earful of this morning's news.

"We just got hit!" Chuck exclaimed as he walked into the house. "Hoop Street, Viola Street, Forty-sixth Street, Fifty-fifth Street, Sixtieth, and Parkside!" he continued.

"Hold da fuck up! What are you talking about?" Hassan asked.

Chuck ran down the strips that had been robbed sometime last night and this morning. "'Bro, three spots got hit this morning. Two last night. Niggas over on Hoop Street said two niggas with bandanas over their faces came through with a shotgun. Mark from Forty-sixth Street said it was a dude and a chick. Back-to-back-to-back. These mothafuckas—"

"Shut da fuck up!" Hassan yelled and grabbed Chuck by the throat and slammed him up against the wall. "All this shit falls back on you! I told you to hold it down, and you said you had it under control. You remember that?" he said through clenched teeth as he squeezed Chuck's throat tighter. "You can't do shit I tell you to do!"

Sarita stood by the kitchen, watching as Hassan chastised Chuck. She couldn't help but laugh on the inside, knowing that the people he identified as the robbers were Mason and Rando. But it was a bit of a surprise when Chuck said that a female was involved. She figured that it had to be Shay getting in on the action. Out of the ten spots Sarita gave Mason to hit last night, five of them were done by this morning, and it wasn't even ten o'clock yet.

Hassan was beyond pissed. Not only did the money spots get hit, but also the dope runners. That was a lot of money and product that was gone, not to mention the fact that without product making it to the strips, dopefiends would more than likely go and find their fix somewhere else, even if that meant going all the way to the other side of the city.

"You listen to me, and listen to me good," Hassan said as he continued squeezing Chuck's neck. "You are gonna go out there and find out who's robbing me, and then you are gonna kill them. I don't give a fuck who they are!" Hassan said in a low voice so only Chuck could hear him. "If you can't do that, you're no good to me!"

No other words needed to be said. Chuck understood that to mean that he too was dispensable. It was clear and unequivocal that he had to find the people behind the robberies. He really didn't know where to start, but he was going to do his best to find out. It was either that or start looking for a plot to be buried.

"Now get da fuck out of my house!"

***

"Nigga, is you sure this information is correct?" Bishop asked, looking down at his boy Mike-Mike's phone.

"Yeah, I'm sure, homie. My BM works in the probation office."

Bishop couldn't believe he was looking at Hassan's whole itinerary for the month according to his probation officer. It showed what days he was going to be taking a urine test, scheduled visits to his attorney, and the four-hour passes he'd be getting Monday through Friday. This information was important to SK because he had been trying to figure out when and where he could kill Hassan. Up until now, Hassan's whereabouts, where he lived, and how he moved were a mystery.

"A'ight, bro, that's wassup!" Bishop said, holding his hand out for a dap. "I'ma make sure the big homie gets you right for this one," he said, the big homie being SK.

Bishop immediately sent an email with all the information about Hassan to his phone. The only thing left to do was get in touch with SK and put a plan in motion.

Nasir dropped Sarita off at the mall as she requested so that she could have some girl time with Shay . . . at least, that was what Sarita told him. She also had to meet up with Hassan today to discuss business.

She stood at the entrance of the mall, waiting for Nasir to pull off, and as soon as he did, she hightailed it across the parking lot to Applebee's, where everybody was supposed to meet up.

"There she goes," Mason announced, giving Sarita a round of applause when she walked up to the table. Shay and Rando playfully got in on the clapping.

Sarita couldn't help but laugh. "Y'all are crazy!" she chuckled, taking a seat at the table. "So how did we make out?"

As instructed by Sarita, they were allowed to count the money without her being there. She trusted everybody at the table.

"Shit, we did good cash-wise. We got a little more than a hundred grand. As for the dope, I didn't count it. Hell, I really don't know how to count that shit anyway," Mason told her.

"Yeah. And what are we supposed to do with all those drugs? We still got that shit from out of Chuck's condo too," Shay cut in.

"Shit, we sell it," Rando suggested.

"Yeah. There's definitely a lot of money involved wit' dat dope. That's more money for us if we can get rid of it," Mason added.

Sarita sat there in deep thought as everybody gave their opinion. She, out of everybody sitting at the table, had the greatest advantage of being able to move the drugs. "Don't worry about the dope. It'll be sold before the week is out," she assured them. "Right now, just focus on the rest of the money that's out there."

Mason, Shay, and Rando looked at one another. They were under the impression that today's events were going to be the end of it. They had more than enough money to go around.

"So how much more are we going to take?" Mason asked. "Not that it matters."

As Sarita stood up to leave, she looked around at everyone, then said, "Until there's nothing left to take."

***

Camille sat in the passenger seat of SK's car, looking out the window at people walking by either going to or coming home from work.

Once Bishop sent SK Hassan's schedule, he jumped at the opportunity to catch him slipping.

"What makes you think he's gonna be here?" Camille asked, looking over at SK.

He sat up in his seat, grabbed his phone out of the center console, and began tapping away at the screen. "You see that building across the street?" he asked her, pointing his finger. "That's the probation office, and from the looks of things, Hassan should be in there right now." He looked down at his phone. "Look, I told you that you don't have to be here. You can take a cab back to the house."

"No. I told you I'm riding out wit' you," Camille reassured him. "So are you going to do that as soon as he walks out of the building?" she asked and pulled out a .99 Taurus from her bag. She didn't care that they were in the middle of downtown, nor did she mind being the one pulling the trigger.

"Nah, it's too risky down here. We're gonna follow him until the right moment. Oh, shit! Look! Look!" SK said while nodding toward the building.

Hassan had emerged and was standing curbside as though he was waiting for a ride.

"Damn! Mike-Mike's baby mom is official!" he said, starting the car.

Through the heavy flow of traffic, a black-on-black Benz S550 pulled up and stopped right in front of Hassan.

"It's go time!" Camille spoke.

SK almost caused an accident when he drove out of his parking spot, trying not to lose Hassan. Center City traffic would definitely be the reason for this type of accident. "They're getting on the expressway. Here, take the wheel. I can do it before they get back to the hood," SK told her. He slowed down so they could make the switch mid-drive, and once Camille was behind the wheel, SK pulled his Glock 9 mm out of the glove compartment. He cocked it back to make sure he had a bullet in the chamber.

Hassan's route was so predictable. The car got off at the Spring Garden exit and headed for West Philly, where it pulled into a gas station and parked beside one of the pumps.

SK set his mind to making it happen there. "Pull up to the driver-side door," he instructed. The plan was simple. He was going to get out, shoot the driver first so they wouldn't be able to pull off, and then empty the rest of the clip into Hassan at close range.

Right at the moment Camille pulled up to the car, the driver-side door opened, and out stepped Sarita. Camille's heart felt like it dropped to the pit of her stomach, and if it weren't for her quick reaction stepping on the gas, SK would have gunned her down.

"What da fuck!" SK yelled, damn near falling out of the car when Camille accelerated. "Turn the car back around!" He could see Hassan getting out of the car to pump the gas.

There was no way in hell Camille was about to follow that order. As badly as she wanted to see Hassan dead, she wasn't willing to have it done with Sarita dying with him. "We gotta do this another time," she said, pulling out of the gas station and into traffic.

SK wasn't trying to hear that. "Stop the fuckin' car!" he yelled again.

"He's got a fuckin' kid in the car! I'm not doing it!" Camille yelled back.

"I don't give a fuck who she is! Turn this muthafuckin' car around!" he ordered, and then pointed his gun at Camille.

Camille pulled the car over to the side of the road and threw the gearshift into park. She had no fear in her eyes when she grabbed the gun sitting on her lap and aimed it at SK.

SK could see in her eyes that she wasn't about to back down.

"What if that were your kid in the car? How would you feel?"

SK just sat there and thought about it. As mad as he was, he couldn't deny that if it were his kid, he would lose it if she were killed accidentally. He lowered his weapon, but Camille kept a firm grip on hers until he fully submitted, which he did.

"A'ight, come on. Let's get out of here," he said, tucking his gun away.

Camille then pulled into traffic.

"A'ight, I only got another hour or so before I gotta head home," Hassan said to Sarita once he got back into the car.

"So where do you want to go now?" Sarita asked.

Hassan sat back in thought. He had been considering the elevation of Sarita within his organization now that Chuck had become unreliable. "What if I told you I could make you rich?" Hassan asked, breaking his silence. "I'm not talking about hood rich, but real rich."

"I don't get it," Sarita said with a curious look on her face.

Hassan took in a deep breath, then exhaled. "I lost over a half million dollars within a week, all under Chuck's watch. My business has become compromised, and I think it's time for a new face."

This was the news Sarita had been waiting for. She knew that there was more to Hassan's business than what she was exposed to thus far. When she said she wanted to bring down his entire operation, this was what she meant.

"Do you think you can handle more responsibility?" Hassan asked.

"If you need me to, I'm willing to learn the game. You know there's a lot I don't know about the dope game."

"Dis shit can get crazy at times, and on any given day, ya life could be in danger."

"I know, and you don't have to worry about that. I can take care of myself."

Hassan always felt that there was something special about her, and with his help, she was going to be exposed to a lifestyle she could never imagine having. It was something he knew how to do well. "Head uptown. I got somebody I want you to meet."

Chapter 12

Grats High School looked like the BET Awards for the 2015 graduation. Hunting Park and Broad Street were jam-packed with luxury cars trying to make their way to the front of the school. It seemed like everybody wanted to stunt hard for their last time at the school.

Sarita, Mason, Rando, and Shay definitely wanted to make a lasting impression, and when they got to the scene, they shut it down.

"Daaaamn!" one onlooker exclaimed while pointing to the all-white Maserati coming through the traffic.

Rando saw some of the freshmen students covering their mouths in awe when he turned into the parking lot. Mason followed up in a tan Aston Martin Rapide, and Shay also had all eyes on her sporting an all-black Bentley GT drop.

But when Sarita bought up the rear, driving a silver McLaren, shit just got real. Even several teachers looked on in shock when they saw all the luxury cars pull up.

The car doors opened, and they all stepped out of their respective cars simultaneously, leaving everybody smiling from ear to ear. It even looked like they were dressed for the BET Awards.

"Damn, we killin' it!" Shay said, walking up next to Sarita.

"Yeah. This is how you make them remember you," Mason added as he and Rando walked over to them.

It wasn't long before crowds of students—mostly friends—gathered around Sarita and her crew. Their iPhones were on deck taking selfies and pictures of the cars. Sarita couldn't help feeling like a celebrity from all the love being shown to her.

"A'ight! A'ight! Break this up!" the vice principal said while making his way through the crowd. "Let's all get inside. The ceremony will be starting shortly," he advised.

The students snapped a few more pictures of the cars before they started to disperse.

"You ready?" Sarita asked Shay with a huge smile on her face.

Shay smiled back, taking in the moment. "Let's do this!"

Camille held on to the dresser with both hands while looking back at SK as she bounced her ass up and down on his dick.

He was lying on the edge of the bed, watching her ass jiggle as she rode him reverse cowgirl. "Damn, girl!"

She sped up, indicating that she was about to cum. The wetter she got, the more SK wanted to bust as well. Her nectar began to ooze from her box, and at the same time his cum shot up inside her. Her legs were shaking and became too weak to stand on, so she sat back and rocked back and forth until SK came.

"Get over here!" he said. He playfully gave her a bear hug and slammed her onto the bed. He lay there spooning with her as his dick remained inside of her. "Ay, I been meaning to holla at you about something," he said, finally pulling his semi-hard dick out of her. "You gon' have to get that girl away from him. Dis shit has to get done like yesterday. And why would she be rolling with him anyway?"

Camille never got into the whole rape situation with SK, mainly because she didn't feel that comfortable sharing that portion of her life with him, at least not this early in the relationship. And as far as the reason why Sarita was with Hassan, Camille had trouble understanding that herself. So many thoughts had run through her mind over the past couple of days, but nothing seemed to make sense. "Well, depending on how Hassan's schedule looked today, you might get what you're asking for," she told SK. "She's graduating today, so more than likely they won't be together."

SK reached over and grabbed his phone from the nightstand. He scrolled through Hassan's schedule and saw that Hassan had a day pass for four hours, and he'd already been out for an hour. There was no telling where he could be because the pass wasn't specific. The only thing SK knew for sure was that Hassan had to go home. He also had Hassan's home address thanks to Mike-Mike's baby mama. SK was thinking about making a house call. "I gotta go," he said, leaning in and kissing Camille. He didn't want to waste another day allowing Hassan to breathe.

"Yeah, I gotta be somewhere too," Camille countered, rolling over and getting out of the bed.

With more than enough on their plates, both Camille and SK got their day started.

Inside the school auditorium, it was standing room only for those who weren't immediate family members of the graduating class. At one point during the ceremony, Sarita had to fight back tears when she looked out into the crowd and saw the empty chairs she had reserved for her family. Her grandmother was in the hospital with the flu, and her grandfather was with her.

Shay's mother, along with other family members of Shay, had come. Mason's parents were there, and Rando's family showed up big for him as well. Hassan and Dion were there too, seeing Nasir off.

"I'm here wit' you, girl," Shay told Sarita, nudging her and grabbing hold of her hand. "We gon' ride it to the end," she assured her.

Hearing those words coming from her best friend melted Sarita's heart, and now she was unable to hold back the tears.

"Congratulations, nephew," Chuck said, shaking Nasir's hand and pulling him in for a hug. "You did it, boy!" he laughed, throwing a few playful jabs. He hadn't thought he'd be in town for the ceremony, but his plans had changed. Hassan threw a couple of jabs too.

"Sarita! Sarita!" Dion yelled, calling her over. "Bring ya friend with you!" Dion didn't want to be completely rude. "Congratulations!" she said, giving Sarita a big hug. She also congratulated Shay, who had walked over with Sarita. "Now where's ya aunt? Finally I can meet her," she said.

Rando and Mason stayed put, noticing that Chuck was there. They really didn't want to take any chances of him knowing who they were. But that decision only made things worse.

Chuck being Chuck felt some type of way that the boys didn't accept Dion's invitation to come over. He walked over to them to try to get them to come to the surprise party they were having for Nasir tonight. "Wassup wit' you two li'l niggas?" he asked them while holding his fist out for some dap.

When he turned to give Rando some dap, Chuck froze. A recap of the robbery at his condo flashed in his mind. His brain locked in on the eyes, which were similar to the eyes he saw looking at him while he was getting robbed. The left eye was slightly lazy just like one of the gunmen's, and upon further examination, he noticed a tattoo on the right side of Rando's neck.

"So look, I got a surprise party for Nasir tonight. How about y'all two coming through? I'll put y'all up in VIP so y'all can do ya thing," Chuck said, not wanting to seem suspicious.

Almost instantly Rando could feel the vibe change, but he played it cool. "Yo, I gotta get back to my family. I'll get the address from Sarita later on," he told Chuck before walking off.

"Yeah, I gotta get out of here too," Mason seconded.

Before Mason walked off, Chuck got a good look at him too. He wasn't sure about Mason because he never got a chance to see the second gunman that night, but he was almost 100 percent sure that Rando was there.

"Bro, I need to holla at you about something," Chuck said to Hassan as he was driving him home.

Hassan didn't respond but continued to listen to Chuck.

"I think I know who robbed me."

Hassan turned around and looked at him, interested in what he had to say.

Chuck had been thinking about this ever since he left the school. It was like he had conjured up a conspiracy theory in his head in a matter of minutes. "I know this shit might sound crazy, but I think . . ."

Thinking about how this was about to sound, he stopped mid-sentence. Aside from the fact that he was talking about some high school kids who had graduated today, he had to worry about how Hassan was going to take the news that his own son's friends were the ones behind the robbery. "You know what, bro? Forget about it. I gotta do some more homework on it."

"Nah, nah, nah. I wanna hear this," Hassan insisted in a sarcastic way.

Chuck definitely wasn't about to say anything now. "It's nothing, bro. I'm just tripping out. Plus, you're home," he said, pulling into Hassan's driveway.

Hassan shook his head. "Bro, you gotta get serious. You really need to get ya shit together. If something happens to me, I'm not even sure you'll be able to hold down my family when I'm gone."

Chuck understood his concerns and didn't have anything to refute them. "I got you, bro. That's my word," he said, holding his hand up for some dap. He was hoping Hassan didn't leave him hanging, and he didn't. That was a relief.

Being home alone was boring as hell, but Hassan worked out to relieve his stress, along with updating the website for his business and taking plenty of naps.

He had only been asleep for a couple of hours before he felt the presence of somebody standing over him. He opened his eyes just in time to see Bishop pull the trigger.

Click!

Hassan jumped, thinking that was it. Fortunately for him, Bishop didn't have a bullet in the chamber. Instinctively Hassan reached for his gun before Bishop could put a round in the chamber.

Bishop punched Hassan in the face and tried to yank the gun out of Hassan's hand.

Hassan wasn't letting go. He held on for dear life and managed to kick Bishop in the stomach. Hassan pulled him down onto the couch, where they began to wrestle. From the couch to the floor, Bishop punched Hassan in his face several times before breaking free. When he backed up and cocked the gun back, Hassan jumped to his feet and took off for the stairs. Bishop let the bullets fly while chasing him.

Pop! Pop! Pop!

The bullets hit the banister, the steps, and the wall going up the stairs.

Pop!

A bullet hit Hassan in the back of his thigh just as he got to the top of the stairs. It didn't faze him due to the amount of adrenaline pumping through his body.

By the time Bishop had gotten to the top of the stairs, Hassan was out of sight. He didn't know what room he disappeared into. He became a little nervous and was tempted to run back down the stairs, but after coming this far, there was no turning back.

He walked down the back hallway toward the room where he thought he'd heard something. When he got up to the door and was about to open it, the hairs on the back of his neck stood up. The presence of somebody standing behind him became obvious, and before he got a chance to turn around, the gun was pressed up against the back of his head. Part of him wanted to beg for his life, but his pride stood in the way of that.

"If you gon' shoot me, then do it, my nigga," he said while clutching the gun he had in his hand a little tighter. He heard the shot but didn't feel anything as the bullet ripped through the back of his head and exited out the side.

His body fell to the floor face-first, and although Hassan wanted to empty the rest of the clip into his body, he reserved his ammo just in case somebody else was either in the house or coming in to help Bishop.

Shay sat on the hood of her Bentley while looking out at the playground. There had to be at least fifty kids running around like they'd just eaten a pound of sugar. The engine from Sarita's McLaren took Shay from her deep thoughts.

"What you thinking about? Having one of those?" Sarita asked when she walked up, referring to the kids.

"Maybe one day. Right now I'm loving my freedom," Shay replied, passing Sarita a bottled water.

Sarita reached into her Louis Vuitton bag, pulled out her phone, then passed Shay the bag.

"What's this?" Shay asked when she took the bag.

"That's the money from the dope. It's one hundred grand. Half for you and half for Mason. I'll take care of Rando when I see him," Sarita replied, taking a seat next to Shay on the car.

It turned out there was over $200,000 in packaged goods that they had taken from Hassan's runners, and because Sarita had a good relationship with Hassan's workers, it wasn't hard to move the product quickly and quietly without Hassan finding out about it.

"What am I supposed to do with all this money?"

"I don't know, girl. Spend it," Sarita shot back. "We didn't have much growing up, but now we good, so just enjoy it. To be honest . . ." Sarita paused while looking at the kids.

Shay nudged her and asked, "What? What are you thinking about?"

Killing Hassan was inevitable and was probably going to happen sooner rather than later. Over the past few days, Sarita got to thinking about her life after the death of Hassan.

"Go ahead and spit it out. I know you wanna say something," Shay encouraged her.

"What if we didn't have to stop right now? I mean, what if I told you that we could be rich?"

Shay held up the Louis Vuitton bag. "What do you call this?" she asked with a smile.

"That's not rich, Shay. That type of money don't last. Do you know that for the first time in my life I counted two million dollars in cash?" Sarita spoke with excitement. "The only problem I had with doing it was that it wasn't my money."

Shay looked over at her. She knew that she already had a plan in mind.

"I'm about to meet one of the biggest heroin dealers in North America. Hassan isn't gonna be around much longer, and once he's gone, the hood is gonna need another supplier."

"And you want to be the one who takes over the city?"

"No. I want *us* to take over the city," Sarita corrected her. Flirting with the street life only brought Sarita closer to the life with every day that went by. She became addicted to hustling and all the fame and power that came along with it. Learning the ropes from Hassan and how to maneuver in the streets gave her the confidence that brought her to this point.

"Shay, I wouldn't ask you to do anything if I didn't think it would be beneficial to you."

Cutting her off, Shay said, "Shut up, girl! You already know that I'm wit' you. Whatever you do, just don't get us killed out here."

Sarita smiled, happy that she had her best friend with her. That was exactly what she needed if she had any plans of being successful. Shay was probably the only person she trusted with her life.

Dion wanted to spend some additional time with Nasir before he was to leave for North Carolina.

"Come on, Mom!" Nasir said when Dion pulled into the Chuck E. Cheese parking lot.

"Boy, don't be faking like you don't want some cheese pizza and some breadsticks."

Chuck E. Cheese was Nasir's favorite place to eat at when he was growing up, and when he stepped out of the car and the scent of pizza hit his nose, he was reminded of how good things were back in those days. "Mom, you crazy!" He smiled, shaking his head.

As they crossed the parking lot, their good mood was interrupted by Chuck speeding through the parking lot and coming to a screeching halt in front of them. Immediately Dion thought that something was wrong with Hassan.

Chuck hopped out of the car as though he was in a hurry. "Wassup, Dion?" he spoke. "Li'l man, I need to holla at you for a second," he said, tapping Nasir's arm.

The two of them walked away, and Dion kept a close eye on them as they talked.

"Ay, I need those spare keys I gave you to my place. Do you got them wit' you?"

"Nah, Unc. The keys are in my room. They're in my nightstand drawer."

"Is there anybody else who has access to them?" Chuck wanted answers, but at the same time, he was checking Nasir's temperature to see if he possibly had anything to do with what was going on. Nobody was ruled out as a suspect.

"Nah, Unc. The keys been in my room since the prom. Why? What's going on?" Nasir questioned.

Chuck's phone vibrating in his pocket caused him to put the lightweight interrogation on hold. "Yo, what up, bro?" he said to Hassan.

"I need you to drop what you're doing and get back over here," Hassan said, then hung up before Chuck could say anything.

From the tone of his voice, Chuck could tell that something was wrong. He headed right back to his car. "Are you sure the keys are still there?" he asked Nasir before he got into the car.

"Yeah, Unc. I'm sure."

Chuck looked over at Dion, who had a concerned look on her face. He let her know that everything was okay, and he would let her know what was going on later. On that, he got into the car and peeled out of the parking lot like a madman.

On her way to the hospital to see her grandmother, Sarita got an urgent call from Hassan saying that she needed to come to his house. As badly as she wanted to decline and see her grandmother anyway, she couldn't. She was at a critical stage in gaining Hassan's trust and was pretty much on call.

"What da fuck is he doing here?" she mumbled to herself when she pulled up to the house and saw Chuck's car sitting in the driveway. She grabbed the Glock .40 from the center console and tucked it into her Gucci bag. She didn't trust Chuck as far as she could throw him, and she wouldn't think twice about putting a bullet in his head if she had to.

"Get in here!" Hassan ordered when he opened the front door. He grabbed her arm and almost pulled it out of the socket when he pulled her into the house. He poked his head out the door and looked up and down the street in a paranoid way before closing the door. "Follow me," he said, walking toward the stairway.

Sarita saw Bishop's body on the floor right at the threshold of Nasir's bedroom. She didn't know that he was dead until she got up close and could see the bullet holes in the back of his head. Chuck suddenly emerged from Nasir's bedroom, startling her.

"I'm gonna need you to help me get rid of the body," Hassan said while looking down at Bishop.

Sarita was still in awe as she gazed at the body. This was the first time she'd ever seen a dead body. To her surprise, it didn't freak her out like she thought it would.

Hassan grabbed Bishop's ankles while Chuck grabbed his upper body. They lifted him up and placed him on a plastic sheet that Hassan had spread out on the floor.

"Before we put this body in the river, we gotta make sure it'll stay in the river. There's an extra-large duffel bag in the closet. Go and get it for me," he instructed Sarita.

These muthafuckas are crazy! Sarita thought while going to the closet.

When she got back, Hassan was in the process of breaking one of Bishop's legs. Sarita cringed at the sound of his bones cracking. At the same time, Chuck was breaking Bishop's arms. They did this to make sure he'd fit into the duffel bag with the weights to sink him to the bottom. This was blowing Sarita's mind, but she stood her ground just as Hassan hoped she would.

Hassan figured that if Sarita could contribute to making the body disappear, she could do anything, which was exactly what he needed.

"I'm telling you, my nigga, he knew it was us," Rando said, pacing back and forth in Shay's living room.

"Calm down, bro. You just paranoid right now. If he even thought it was us, he would have made a move. Now cool out and blow some of this weed."

"Yeah, 'cause you making me nervous," Shay chimed in.

Rando heard both Mason's and Shay's responses, but he wasn't feeling it. He could see in Chuck's eyes that he knew something, and a vicious confrontation happening was the only thing Rando could think about. "Look, I don't know about y'all, but I'm tryin'a go and handle this shit before it gets out of hand." He grabbed his gun off the coffee table and stuffed it in his waistband.

Shay stopped him before he could walk out the door. A part of her felt where he was coming from, but she wasn't trying to make a move until she talked to Sarita and got her opinion about the situation. Rando agreed.

Shay grabbed her phone immediately. "Can you talk right now?" she asked when Sarita answered the phone.

Aside from Sarita driving down the highway with a dead body in the car, sitting in the passenger seat was Chuck, whom she didn't feel comfortable talking around. She cut her eyes over at him to see if he was watching her. At the same time, he was cutting his eyes over at her. "Yeah, now is not a good time," she replied.

Shay had Sarita on speaker, so Rando said what he had to say. "Ay, Sarita, I think da nigga Chuck knows it was us!"

Sarita cut her eyes over at Chuck again, hoping that he didn't hear anything that was being said. It didn't appear that he did. "A'ight, I'll be there in an hour," she said, and hung up before Rando could say anything else.

SK tried over and over again to call Bishop's phone. The call kept going straight to voicemail. All kinds of thoughts ran through his mind.

"I told you that it wasn't a good idea," Camille said from the couch.

SK stood by the window with his phone in his hand and periodically looked down the street for any cars to come through. He was beginning to regret sending his boy on that mission. He tried calling and calling but still got the same results.

He was just about to give up, but he dialed Bishop's number again, and it began to ring once, twice, and on the third ring, someone picked up. There was silence, but he could hear someone breathing on the other end. "Yo, my nigga!" he said, and got no response for a moment.

"So it was you this whole time trying to kill me!" Hassan said, breaking the silence.

SK paused, figuring that if Hassan answered the phone, then more than likely Bishop was dead. He bit down on his lip in anger, and Hassan confirmed the outcome he expected.

"If you tryin' to talk to Bishop, he zipped up at the moment." Hassan laughed. "He's all broken up not being able to speak. But you'll talk again when I kill you too."

SK wished that he could reach through the phone and choke Hassan to death. Being that he couldn't, he wanted to give Hassan a stern warning as to what was coming. He said just a few words, but a few words with weight. "I'ma kill you!"

Chapter 13

Chuck rode around the city all day, checking up on all the trap houses that got hit earlier in the week. It wasn't for the purpose of making sure that the dope made it to its respected strips, but more so to put the rest of the pieces of the puzzle together. Every spot was hit at different times, but with the same MO. In one case, one of the workers noticed a similar scar over the eyes of one of the gunmen.

"Yo, my niece Tasha said that she knows everybody in this picture," Moe said to Chuck while sitting in the passenger seat. He had his niece on the phone and put it on speaker so that Chuck could hear her.

Chuck was so excited he had to pull over. Moe's niece was only in the tenth grade, but she knew all the popular kids in school.

"It's Mason, Sarita, Shay, and Randy," Tasha said.

"Randy?" Chuck asked.

"Yeah. But they call him Rando," Tasha explained.

"Tell me that you know where they be at," Chuck said, praying that she did.

"I only know where Mason lives because he lives on my grandmother's street."

"That's on Norris Street," Moe cut in.

This was the break Chuck was looking for. "Good lookin' out, baby girl."

Moe hung up the phone. Not that he didn't know what was to come, but he had to ask. "So how you gonna handle it?"

Chuck still wasn't 100 percent sure that Mason had anything to do with the robbery, but his gut told him that Sarita had everything to do with it. When he was at Hassan's house dealing with the Bishop situation, he checked Nasir's nightstand and found that the keys to his condo weren't there like Nasir had told him. The only other person who had access to the keys and had the potential to do something grimy with them was Sarita. Because they were all friends and seemed to be cool at the graduation, he was going to check the temperature of everybody.

Sarita looked bossy when she pulled up to the Manyunk Golf Club in the McLaren. She stepped out wearing a cream-colored linen suit, showing off her lace bikini. On her feet was a pair of gold Jimmy Choo sandals.

"Mr. Torres has been expecting you," a staff member said while holding out his arm to escort her inside.

The valet bowed to her before running around to the driver side of her car and getting in. This was the first time she'd been given the VIP treatment.

"*Hola, mami!*" Torres greeted her, getting up from the table as Sarita approached.

She was in awe but had to keep her composure and at least look like she was somebody who was in charge. "*Como esta? Que tu hesse?*" she greeted him, extending her hand. "Please, let's sit," she said.

"Wow! Hassan didn't tell me how beautiful you are. I was expecting someone a little more hood." Torres smiled.

"I'm flattered, but with all due respect, I'd like to get straight to business," Sarita said. "Hassan sends his apologies for not being able to be here. As you know, he has some legal issues he's dealing with. For now, I'll be running point on the business aspect."

Torres was feeling Sarita and the way she was handling herself, and just like she had suggested, it was time to get down to business. "Okay, talk money," he said, leaning back in his chair and crossing his legs.

"Well, as you know, Hassan sent me here with two and a half million dollars. But I have some of my own money as well. I understand Hassan never spent more than two million dollars at a time with you—"

"How much of your own money do you have?" Torres cut in.

"I have two and a half million dollars as well, and I'm willing to spend it all with you just as long as you can supply me with the best-quality product, and for the best price."

"You have five million dollars here with you today?"

"Give me a good number, Mr. Torres, or I can spend the normal two million as instructed by Hassan."

Torres looked out at the golf course for a minute. $2 million was okay, but $5 million sounded even better. "I'm prepared to go as low as forty-five grand a kilo if you can guarantee me a shipment like this every month."

Sarita was good with numbers, and the return investment was lucrative. The only thing she wasn't sure of was how fast she could get rid of the product. Hassan was soon to be out of the way, and getting rid of that much dope was going to take a lot of hard work and dedication. After thinking about it for a hot second, she was in.

***

SK sat on the edge of the bed, flicking through the channels in order to catch the news. He been on the look-out for Bishop's body to turn up, but so far there was nothing. Every time his phone rang, he thought that it was going to be the call he was looking for. It was important to him that Bishop's death was confirmed so that he could have a proper burial.

If Hassan hadn't up and moved out of his house, SK would have firebombed it, waited for Hassan to run out of the house, and then put a bullet in his head. That was how much anger and pain he felt about losing his best friend.

"Baby, you gotta eat something," Camille said, walking into the room with a plate of food in her hand.

SK was so discombobulated that he hadn't realized that it had been forty-eight hours since he'd eaten anything. "Yo, I need you to keep a low profile for a couple of days. Shit is about to get crazy, and I really don't want you around," he said with a serious look on his face. "I need to find out where that muthafucka is resting his head, and the only way I can do that is if I—"

"I might be able to help you with that. I know the girl who was with Hassan that day at the gas station."

SK looked over at her.

"I know. I know. I'm sorry. I just know the girl from my old neighborhood. Her mother still lives around there," Camille lied.

"Babe, I'm not gonna lie. That would be a big help. See what you can do for me."

Camille paused, thinking about her relationship with her daughter and how she wanted to trust SK enough to tell him her whole life story. It was still too early, and she wasn't sure if he would understand it. "I got you, babe. Let me make a few calls and see what I can do. I can't promise you anything though."

"I know, but can you at least try?" SK asked, looking up at her with the most sorrowful eyes.

"Baby, I got you," Camille responded, and kissed his forehead.

SK was sick about Bishop, and he wasn't going to rest without either finding him or finding Hassan, which was just as good.

"Damn! Dis nigga is getting some major money!" Moe said, watching Mason hop out of his Aston Martin. The intel that Tasha gave was on point, and it only took about twenty minutes before Mason pulled up to his grandmother's house, got out of his car, and entered the house.

"Stay right here. I'll be right back," Chuck said, stepping out of his car. The twenty to thirty kids running up and down the street made a good cover, allowing Chuck to walk up the steps and onto the porch without even being noticed. He was right on time, too.

When Chuck got up to the door, Mason was opening the door to leave the house. But when he saw Chuck, he knew what it was. He didn't have time to react. Chuck had his gun pointed right at his chest, causing him to back up into the house.

"Mason, are you still downstairs?" Ms. Gloria, Mason's grandmother, called from upstairs.

"Yeah, Grandma, I'm down here. Stay upstairs though because I have company," Mason yelled back.

Chuck pushed Mason backward onto the couch, but not before a quick pat down. Mason now regretted leaving his gun in his car.

"Where da fuck is my money?" Chuck demanded.

"I don't know what you're talking about," Mason answered, holding his hands up.

"You must think I'm a fuckin' fool. I know about you and ya boy, Rando, and that bitch, Sarita. Y'all must think I'm sweet."

Over the past few days, Chuck had put everything together, or at least he thought he had. Sarita was one of the few people who knew routes, houses, and locations where the money and dope were to be picked up or dropped off. On several occasions, the trap houses got robbed moments before she got there, and on at least one occasion, a robbery happened while she was there. It was the robbery of Chuck's condo that linked everything and everyone together. In addition to the unique scar on Rando's face, which Chuck was sure he identified, Sarita was the only person from the hood who knew where Chuck lived, and she had the opportunity to get the keys to his place. He figured Sarita saw how good he was living the night Nasir took her there, and then decided to rob him. Rando and Mason were the closest things to thugs Sarita had around, and the most obvious ones to put in work.

"Give me my fuckin' money or I'ma call ya grandmother down here and shoot her in the face right in front of you!" Chuck threatened. He was dead serious, too.

Mason, on the other hand, wanted to try his hand one last time before caving into his demands. "I told you, I don't—"

"Grandma!" Chuck yelled out, taking the safety off his gun.

"Okay! Okay!" Mason complied, not wanting anything to happen to his grandmother. "I don't have all of it, but I can get you the rest." He slowly got up off the couch and headed for the basement.

Chuck was right behind him with the gun pointed at his back. "Do one thing stupid and I'ma kill you!" he warned.

Once downstairs, Mason hit the stash spot that was behind the bar. Chuck watched and was on go if Mason acted like he wanted to play Superman.

"This is all I got," Mason said and handed a black leather bag to Chuck. "There's like a hundred grand there, and like I said, I'll get you the rest."

Chuck opened the bag and saw the money. It wasn't what he wanted, but it was enough. He took a step back and pointed the gun at Mason.

"Come on, man! I gave you what I got, and I didn't try anything stupid!" Mason pled, not wanting to die.

"You did do something stupid the night you robbed me."

Pop!

The bullet hit Mason in his chest, knocking him backward to the ground. Chuck walked over, stood over him, and let off several more shots.

Pop! Pop! Pop! Pop!

"Grandma, I'm pulling up to the hospital now," Sarita spoke into the phone. She had almost forgotten that Mrs. Scott was getting discharged today. Her grandfather was the one who had reminded her.

Sarita went straight to the hospital after meeting with Torres, so there wasn't any time to switch cars. When she pulled up and double-parked the McLaren in front of the hospital, as always, heads turned. It took a few minutes before Mrs. Scott emerged from the hospital, and Sarita instantly became irritated at the sight of Camille, who was pushing her wheelchair.

"How in the world am I supposed to ride in this?" Mrs. Scott said, looking at the two-seater.

"Aw, Mom, she's taking you home in style," Camille cut in.

Sarita knew Camille all too well and knew that she wasn't there out of the kindness of her heart. "What are you doing here?" she asked her as she helped her grandmother into the car.

Camille paused, still a little shocked at the vehicle upgrade. "I really need to talk to you."

"What could we possibly have to talk about?" Sarita shot back.

Camille waited until Mrs. Scott was in the car before she began. "I saw you with him the other day. Why are you hanging with Darnell or Hassan or whatever he calls himself these days, after knowing who he is?"

"It's none of your business, but if you must know, I'm doing to him what you should have done eighteen years ago."

"You think killing anybody is easy? You think you're 'bout that life?" Camille asked.

Sarita looked right back at her. But this time there was something in Sarita's eyes that caused Camille to change her opinion. "You look at me and tell me if you really think I'm capable of murder," Sarita said with a strong voice.

Knowing the kind of man Hassan was, Camille imagined that murder could easily be running through her blood. The one thing Camille had to admit was this wasn't the same Sarita she once knew. She had grown up and become a woman, and from the looks of things, she was able to stand on her own two feet. Camille was a little jealous, too. "So can we get together later? I still need to talk to you."

Sarita walked around to the driver-side door and opened it. Dealing with or even talking to Camille was the last thing on her mind. She really didn't have much to say. "See you in traffic, Camille!" she said, and then got into her car and pulled off.

Chapter 14

"Get in here. Did you make sure nobody was following you?" Hassan asked Chuck when he entered the house.

"Nah, wasn't nobody following me. But check dis out. I found the muthafuckas who been robbing us," Chuck said. "And you're not gonna believe dis shit."

Chuck took a seat on the couch and started to give his spiel just as Sarita walked out of the kitchen. She overheard what Chuck said and gave him a devious look before she too took a seat on the couch. There was an awkward moment when Chuck and Sarita stared at each other.

With the two staring at each other with uneasy eyes, Hassan took notice. "What da fuck is up wit' y'all two?" he asked, looking back and forth at them.

Chuck was about to say something, but Hassan's phone began vibrating on the coffee table. He looked at the screen and saw that it was Torres. "I gotta take this," he said, taking the phone into the other room.

"Bitch, I know about you!" Chuck whispered, looking back to see where Hassan was.

"And I know about you too. Buying dope from the same person who's trying to kill ya brother. What do you think he's gonna do to you when he finds out?" Sarita taunted.

"Bitch, I should kill you right now!" Chuck snapped, pulling the compact .45 from his hip.

"You not gonna do shit. You kill me and I guarantee Hassan finds out about you and Dion before the end of the day," Sarita said. She reached into her bag, pulled out her cell phone, and showed him a picture of him and Dion walking hand in hand through the front doors of the Holiday Inn. "You might as well dig ya grave right next to mine," she continued, and quickly put her phone back into her bag before Hassan walked back into the room.

Chuck tucked his .45 back into his pocket, seeing that Sarita had the upper hand on him. The information she had was a sure death sentence, brother or not.

"What da hell is going on wit' y'all two?" Hassan asked again when he sat back down on the couch. The tension in the room was thick.

"Nah, everything's good," Chuck replied.

"Good, 'cause Poppy got it in. Sarita, you're gonna make the pickup—"

"Hold up, brah! You gonna trust her wit' all that product?" Chuck protested. "I can handle it."

Hassan turned around and looked at Chuck like he was crazy. "Nigga, if I thought you was responsible enough to make the pickup, you'd be doing it. But being that I don't have that much confidence in you, Sarita's gonna run point on this one."

Chuck was really pissed off, and Sarita sitting there with a smirk on her face made it even harder for him not to blow a gasket. He gave Hassan a look of disappointment before getting up and leaving the house.

Hassan felt bad for about ten seconds and then got right back to business. "The pickup is at ten o'clock tonight. Don't fuck dis up," he told Sarita before dismissing her.

At first Camille didn't think that Sarita was going to show up, but when she walked through the doors, a sigh of relief came over her. "Thank you for meeting up with me," Camille said.

Camille's humble vibe was kind of throwing Sarita off. She'd never seen her like this. "Well, you said that this was important."

"I know, and it is. I really want to warn you about being around Darnell the way you are—"

"His name is Hassan," Sarita corrected her.

"Yeah, well, Hassan killed somebody very important the other day, and I don't want you to be around when the shit hits the fan."

As Camille was talking, Sarita was trying to figure out who she was talking about. Then it hit her. "You're not talking about Bishop, are you?" she asked.

Camille was shocked that Sarita knew. "Yeah, Bishop. How did you know about that? If you know anything, I need you to tell me."

"Tell you? Why would I do that?"

Camille was almost ready to go back to her ghetto side when she heard the bass in Sarita's voice. She caught herself, knowing she wasn't going to get anything accomplished that way. "Bishop was my boyfriend's best friend, and all they want now is to know where his body is so they can give him a proper burial."

Sarita just sat there thinking.

"I hope that man didn't turn you heartless the way he is. I know you, Sarita, and that's not the kind of person you are."

"You don't know me!" Sarita snapped. "I'm not a little girl anymore. I've changed, and if you were any kind of mother the way you were supposed to have been, you would know that about me." She began gathering her things so she could leave.

Camille was actually starting to feel bad. "Sarita, can you please not do this? Please!" Camille practically shouted before Sarita got up.

People in the restaurant cut their eyes at the two, curious as to what was going on.

Seeing the desperation in Camille's eyes, Sarita sat back down. Aside from the fact that Sarita knew that Camille was running game, she was right about her heart not being cold as Hassan's, at least not yet.

"Ya friend Bishop is buried in the deepest waters of Cobbs Creek Park. The stream runs about fifteen miles long, so tell ya friend he's gonna need a wetsuit," Sarita informed her. She could have been a little more specific about the whereabouts of Bishop's body, but she wanted Camille to work for it.

"Thank you," Camille said.

Sarita got up and walked off.

Camille jumped right on the phone and called SK. "I got some good news, baby. I'm on my way to you," she told him, then gathered her things to leave.

Little did she know, SK had somebody tailing her and already knew where she was and who she was meeting with. It wasn't that he didn't trust her, but rather he'd hoped that Camille would lead him to the young girl who was in the car with Hassan. Once he had that information, he was going to do the rest. And finding out where Hassan was resting his head was inevitable.

***

Thinking about the conversation she had with Shay about getting into the dope game, Sarita knew that several factors needed to be considered before she herself committed 100 percent. Safety and security was the number one priority. She didn't have an army of a vicious crew behind her to hold it down if things got crazy. Neither she nor Shay had ever shot anybody in their lives, let alone killed anybody. Mason and Rando had a couple of shootings under their belts and a few robberies, but in the bigger scheme of things, that alone wasn't going to be enough. "What am I getting myself into?" she questioned herself.

Then there was the supplier, which was the next part of the takeover. Torres was cool, and Sarita made a lasting impression on him when she made the $5 million deal, but Torres might not go with the whole takeover plan, and it was very likely he could show his loyalty to Hassan and tell him, which would lead to Sarita's death. But it was a chance worth taking.

Sarita looked down at her phone and was hesitant to make the call. Without him being on board, her entire plan would be in vain.

She sat there contemplating and came to the conclusion that she had come too far to turn back now. She scrolled through her phone list until she came to Torres's number. When she called, he picked up on the first ring. It was as if he knew she was calling.

"*Hola, mami! Como esta?*" he greeted her, sitting back in his chair.

"*Bien, papi. Yo tango que ablar contigo,*" she said, letting Torres know that she needed to talk to him.

He was intrigued. "I'll be playing golf until around six o'clock. I'll see you when you get here."

Chapter 15

Mason's funeral was the next day, and Shay didn't leave the house to do anything. If it weren't for Sarita bringing her food every day, she probably wouldn't have eaten. All of this was devastating and didn't make things any easier.

"Here she go right here," Rando said, standing by the window and watching as Sarita was pulling up.

"Just let me talk to her. She'll do it if I ask her to," Shay said.

Sarita could feel something was up the moment she walked through the door. "What are y'all up too?" she asked while putting the McDonald's bag on the table.

Rando couldn't help himself and blurted out, "We need to kill dat muthafucka!"

He and Shay had been contemplating that since yesterday. He was sure that Chuck was the one behind Mason's death.

"Look, I know how y'all feel, but if we do anything right now, it's gonna fall back on us," Sarita advised.

"Be smart. Dat nigga knows it was us. I'm not tryin'a sit around and wait for him to kill me next," Rando countered.

"We don't have time to waste. He killed Mason. It's Mason!" Shay cried out.

"Yeah, that muthafucka killed my boy!" Rando added.

"All right!" Sarita shouted, feeling their frustration.

Rando hissed, hoping that he could be a part of the move.

Sarita could see that her remarks weren't convincing. "Look at me," she demanded, looking back and forth from Shay to Rando. "I said let me take care of it." The conviction in her voiced sounded real, and for that, Shay knew that the deed was going to get done.

Rando, on the other hand, wasn't too sure. He was literally living in fear and wanted to eliminate the threat. He was only going to give Sarita one chance to get it done, and if she didn't handle it, he damn sure was going to.

"You can't be serious. How da hell does she know?" Dion asked, looking across the table at Chuck in shock.

"I don't know. The li'l bitch got pictures and everything," Chuck said, shaking his head. "And she seems to have Hassan wrapped around her li'l finger, too. I'd kill her, but who knows what she did with those pictures?"

The pictures were definitely a problem for Dion. It was the end of her marriage for sure, and depending on the way Hassan would feel if he found out, it could also mean the end of her life, and she knew it. "He cannot find out about us!" Dion said, becoming scared at the thought of it. "You gotta do something."

Chuck got up from the table and knelt down in front of her. "He's not gonna find out. I'ma do whatever I gotta do to make sure those pictures never make it into his hands. Look at me," he said, turning her face to his. "I got you." He stood up and grabbed her hand. He led Dion to his bedroom, and when she got to the door, she attempted to resist. But Chuck knew how to weaken her. He smacked the side of her face, which made her smack him back. He grabbed her by the throat and slammed her up against the door, reaching around and unzipping her skirt.

"Stop! Don't do this!" Dion whined.

Chuck leaned in and began to kiss her. It lowered her guard, and within moments, she became submissive and allowed him to remove her blouse. He knew just the way she liked it: rough, trashy, and dominating. "You want dis dick! Tell me you want this dick!"

When Dion refused to say it, he reached down and grabbed two handfuls of her ass and lifted and parted it. Dion's pussy quickly got wet.

"Tell me you want dis dick!" he said in a sterner way.

Dion began to unfasten his belt while kissing his chest. He had his hooks in her, and at that moment, she caved.

Cobbs Creek Park stretched for about fifteen miles, and with the thick brush, unlevel terrain, and bugs flying around everywhere, the conditions in the park made it hard to maneuver. SK wasn't about to let any of that deter him from searching every inch of the creek. He brought his crew with him. There were about twenty people in all.

"I swear to God he'd better be in here," SK said to Camille while looking out at the flowing stream. He walked into the waist-high water, beginning his search. He was followed by several others who didn't seem to have a problem with the water either. "Spread out and call me if you find him!" he shouted so everybody could hear him.

Camille stood on the bank, watching. The efforts of everybody else made her want to join in. She took one deep sniff of the creek water, tied up her sneakers, and jumped in.

Sarita pulled up to the Cedar Hill Condos and looked around at all the luxury cars sitting pretty in their reserved parking spots. Today she was looking to see about getting her own place, and of course it was far away from the city. She'd been staying in hotels from Atlantic City to Philly, and though it was nice and quiet in the hotels, there was nothing like having a place to call home.

"Hi! I'm so glad you could make it," Anne, a tall white blonde, said to her when she got out of the car.

"Hey, Anne. I hope I can get one of these reserved parking spots too," Sarita said, still looking around the parking lot.

"Hell, you can have one right next to me if you like," Anne joked but was serious at the same time. "Now I have three units to show you, so let's get to it."

Sarita followed Anne while she explained the history of the condominiums and some of the famous residents who lived there. This wasn't the average condo, so the security was tight. People needed to have identification on them at all times once inside the building.

"I think you're going to love this one," Anne said, opening up the front door to the first condo.

The first thing Sarita noticed was the breathtaking view of the forest, complemented by the Pocono Mountains in the distance.

The condo itself looked just as good as the view. There were hardwood floors, panoramic windows, marble countertops, his-and-hers walk-in closets, and a master bedroom with a Jacuzzi and a five-by-seven walk-in shower in the bathroom.

"Damn! Can it really get any better than this?" Sarita asked, coming out of the master bedroom.

Anne smiled. "This is the cheapest condo on the market right now."

"And what's the asking price on this one?" Sarita asked.

"A half million dollars."

Sarita wasn't surprised by the number. The other two condos she was supposed to check out were in the price range of a million dollars, which was an amount she knew she couldn't afford right now. Even five hundred grand was pushing it. "I have four hundred and fifty thousand dollars right now, in cash," she proposed.

Usually Anne wasn't in the business of negotiating, but for some reason she liked Sarita. "Four eighty," she countered.

"Four seventy-five," Sarita offered, and reached into her Louis Vuitton bag and pulled out one of the wads of money she had.

Anne would be taking a hit on her commission, but a sale on her record would look good to her boss. "You know what? You—"

Before Anne could finish her statement, Sarita's phone began to ring in her pocket. Hassan's number popped up on the screen. "Excuse me, I have to take this," she said and walked off into the other room. "Yeah, wassup?" she answered, looking out the living room window.

"Look. I'ma send Chuck wit' you tonight. I want you to be safe," Hassan told her. Despite the lack of trust he had in Chuck, Hassan knew that he would make sure the transaction was safe and secure. If Chuck was good at anything, it was getting $2 million across state lines.

"A'ight. I'll stop by and pick him up tonight," Sarita told him and then hung up the phone.

She walked back into the room where Anne was stand-ing, took another look around, and stuck her hand out. "Sounds like four seventy-five is a deal. Draw up the pa-perwork, and let's have a signing over lunch tomorrow," she said with a smile.

The sun was starting to go down, and SK was only about halfway through the creek. Certain parts of the stream weren't that deep, while other parts were just too muddy to see the bottom. There were also some deeper parts of the creek that smelled like shit, which everybody hated to go near.

"Babe, you wanna finish this tomorrow?" Camille asked, walking up behind SK along the side of the bank.

SK reached up and was pulled up onto the bank by his boy. But by no means was he ready to leave. "I don't give a fuck if it takes all night. We gonna clear this whole creek," he told Camille with conviction. "Did you call that girl back like I asked you to?" he halfway snapped. "She can save us all—"

"I tried to call, but she's not answering the phone."

"Well, keep trying!" he turned around and yelled at her. He could see by the look on her face that he'd scared the hell out of her, which was something he never wanted to do. "Damn, babe! My bad!" he said, reaching out to console her. "I'm just stressed da fuck out right now."

"You don't have to explain. I know you're going through a lot."

"SK! Yo, SK!" one of his boys yelled out from about twenty-five yards upstream.

SK took off running, and if it weren't for his wet clothes weighing him down, he would have gotten there faster.

Bear was standing in about five feet of murky water about a few feet from the bank. "Yo, I feel something big down here. Like some kind of bag."

SK jumped into the water, and as soon as he got up to Bear, he could feel the large bag under his feet. It was as if he knew that it was Bishop. He took a deep breath and went under. A few seconds later he pulled up the heavy bag and dragged it over to the bank. It was so heavy that Bear had to help him heave it out of the water. Everyone who was there stood around SK and waited for him to open it.

The stench of the decaying body wafted out of the bag when he opened it. Heads turned at the smell. Inside was Bishop for sure, and four sixty-pound dumbbells.

He sat there in the grass staring at his best friend. It was difficult for him to process seeing his decaying friend. SK didn't want to believe it. He couldn't stop thinking about how much he would miss him.

Dion walked out onto the deck, where Hassan was sitting in a lounge chair with a glass of scotch in his hand. Holding on to lies was beginning to weigh her down. "I have to tell you something." She took a seat at the foot of the chair.

Hassan put the glass of scotch down on the table next to him, then pulled her to his chest. "What did I do now?" He kissed her on the shoulder.

Dion knew she wasn't going to be able to hold on to this lie forever, and she definitely didn't want him to hear it from somebody else. "Baby, I'm sorry." Her eyes began to water.

Hassan quickly got serious and wiped the single tear that rolled down her face. "Damn, Dee! What's going on?" he asked.

One look into his eyes made her think about what she was about to do.

"What are you thinking about?" Hassan asked.

Dion was beginning to have second thoughts.

"What's wrong, bae?" Hassan asked again, snapping Dion out of her train of thought.

Sitting there wrapped in his arms was like torture. She had to say something. She wanted to lie but couldn't think fast enough. The knot in her throat almost choked her. "I wanted—"

"Damn, bro!" Chuck yelled as he came from around the side of the house and into the backyard. "I been ringing ya bell and calling ya phone for the past five minutes," he complained, coming up onto the deck.

Dion capitalized on Chuck's appearance and whispered in Hassan's ear, "We'll talk later." She got up and went into the house.

"My bad if I interrupted anything," Chuck said.

Hassan was concerned about what Dion had on her mind. Unfortunately, now wasn't the time to pry. Transporting one hundred kilos of heroin back into Pennsylvania was his top priority. This shipment was going to determine whether he could keep control over his section of the city.

"Whatever you do, just don't lose them," Detective White told his partner, Detective Smith, as they followed Sarita. Traffic in the city was a little rough, and trying to keep up with them had become difficult.

"You don't want me to pull them over?" Smith asked. The frustration in his voice was clear to Detective White.

Sarita maneuvered the SUV through traffic as though she were riding a dirt bike. It was like she knew she was being followed.

"Nah, don't pull them over. I don't wanna tip them off that we're watching them. There's something about that girl. I got a feeling Hassan's using her for something. We just have to be patient and wait for her to make a mistake."

Ever since Detective White had the meeting with the Feds and found out that Hassan was a part of a major drug investigation, he took more of an interest in helping the Feds bring Hassan to justice.

"Ah, shit! I think we're going to lose her!" Smith said, seeing how far back he was. "The traffic lights are changing. What do you want me to do?" In order to stay behind her, Smith knew that he would have to push through traffic before he reached the light.

Sarita went through the light as it was turning red, and the detectives knew they had to do something.

"You want me to hit the light?" Smith asked. His window of opportunity was about to close.

White had to weigh his options quickly. "Nah, let her go. We'll try to catch up to her at the next light."

Smith watched as the SUV went deeper and deeper into traffic. When the light turned green, he tried to speed down the street to catch up with her, but the SUV was gone.

The Cadillac truck was the transport vehicle and could store the one hundred kilos of heroin they were picking up. Sarita drove while Chuck played the passenger side the whole ride there. It was silent. No radio, no phones, and definitely no conversation.

"A'ight, get off the next exit," Chuck said and checked his rearview.

"That's not the route Hassan told me to take. I'm supposed to take 10."

"This is a faster route. We'll get there a little earlier," Chuck said.

Even if that were the case, Sarita didn't trust him one bit and wasn't about to go off course with him, especially while they were alone. "If you got a problem with the route, then call Hassan," she shot back in a smart way.

Chuck was hot, but he didn't say anything more. He cracked a wicked smile and then focused back on the road.

Sarita kept driving, getting off at the exit she was supposed to, then pulling over to the side of the road about a mile away from the location. Chuck opened the stash spot in the glove compartment and grabbed his gun. Sarita did the same, grabbing her gun from the door panel. When they both got out of the truck and walked to the back, Chuck looked around and thought that this would be a good time to put a bullet in the back of Sarita's head. The only thing stopping him was the pictures she had in her phone. He wasn't sure if she had them stored somewhere else, so keeping her alive was his best option for now.

"When we get up there, I don't need you to say anything," Sarita told him as she opened the back door. "When I tell you to, just grab the dope and put it in the car."

Chuck was frustrated hearing Sarita talk to him in that manner. He could only grin and bear it. "Have fun, 'cause this will be ya last time making a move like this!" he spat. He became tempted again to put that bullet in the back of her head.

They both grabbed the duffle bags from the back of the truck.

Sarita got back into the SUV, and within minutes she was pulling into the industrial site where Torres was waiting. He had several men standing there with him, all holding fully automatic weapons.

"*Hola, mami!*" Torres greeted her when Sarita got out of the SUV.

"*Como esta?*" she said, returning the greeting. She walked over to him and shook his hand.

Chuck grabbed the two duffle bags and waited off to the side while she and Torres had a conversation. "Yeah, bitch! You'll be good and dead by tomorrow!" he mumbled to himself.

Sarita looked over and gave Chuck a nod to make the exchange with Torres's workers.

"You know that once you go down this road, there's no coming back," Torres warned her as they both watched Chuck load the truck.

"I know. I think it's time for some changes within this organization, *papi. El espero se acabo,*" Sarita replied.

Torres nodded his head in agreement. He could see it wasn't looking good for Hassan. He was either going to be killed or end up in prison, the former being more certain. Torres was going to have to continue his business in Philly. A lot of his wealth depended on it. He could see that Sarita was the perfect successor. She had a solidified future as a new and young up-and-coming boss. The sky was the limit. "Let me see you work," he said, nodding to one of his men.

Sarita walked over to Chuck while he was loading the dope. She waited until he put the last kilo into the stash, then pulled the gray and black .45 semiautomatic from her waistband. When Chuck locked the compartment and closed the back door, he turned around only to see Sarita's gun pointed at his face. He didn't seem intimidated. He simply looked at her like she was crazy.

"Now you gotta pull the trigger, because if you don't—"

Pop!

A single bullet hit Chuck in the center of his forehead at point-blank range, knocking him back onto the SUV. He slid to the ground as blood flowed from the gaping wound in the back of his skull. Sarita stood over him and squeezed the trigger, sending another hot lead ball into his head. She made sure there was no coming back for him, not in this lifetime anyway.

Torres was going to make sure the body was never found.

Shay was taking a catnap on the couch when she was awakened by the screen door being unlocked. She slid her hand under the cushions and pulled out a P80 Ruger. She jumped up with the gun in her hand and ducked behind the couch.

When Sarita walked through the front door, Shay let out a sigh of relief. "Girl, you scared the shit out of me!" Shay said, standing up behind the couch. She walked over and turned the lights on, and the first thing she noticed was the gun Sarita had in her hand. She could tell that something had happened.

Sarita walked over and placed her gun on the coffee table, then flopped down on the couch while thoughts of Chuck flashed through her mind. He was the first person she had ever killed, and it weighed on her heart. "It's done," she said, laying her head on Shay's shoulder.

Nothing more needed to be said. Shay understood that Sarita had killed Chuck. She began stroking Sarita's hair, not wanting to imagine how hard that must have been for her. "You did it for us, and I thank you for that. I don't know if I would have had the guts to do something like that," she said.

"And I would never want you to. I would never want you to feel the way I feel right now. I'm not even the same person. I'm just as bad as my—"

"You're nothing like him," Shay cut her off.

Sarita didn't believe it. Some of the anger and violence she saw Hassan display on a regular basis had resonated in her heart, and oftentimes it would show its ugly head in her behavior. The disregard for human life and the hunger for money and power were starting to take form in her thoughts. She wasn't quite the same as Hassan, but she wasn't too far off. In time her true colors would show, and nothing in this world would be able to stop it.

Chapter 16

SK cracked open his eyes after hearing a bunch of little kids playing outside his car. It was morning, and after driving around all night and smoking blunt after blunt, he found himself parked right in front of Bishop's mom's house. He'd given her his word that as soon as he heard from Bishop, he would let her know. Telling her that he was dead would be the hardest thing he ever had to do, which was why he just now found the strength to get out of his car. The walk from his car to the front door felt like walking the Green Mile.

But little did he know that Ms. Grace was sitting in the window watching him the entire time and had been most of the night. Seeing his demeanor, she knew that something was wrong. She opened the door expecting to hear the worst, and SK didn't disappoint.

"Ms. Grace," he began after they entered the house. He looked over at the mantel and saw a picture of him and Bishop. This caused him to break down. He cried like no other, falling to his knees and planting his face in his hands.

Ms. Grace covered her mouth and looked to the sky as her eyes began to fill with tears.

Bishop's sister came down the steps, and when she saw SK on his knees and her mother on the couch in tears, she knew something was wrong with Bishop. "Where is he?" she cried out. "Where is my brother?" Getting nothing but loud cries in return, she began to cry too. She became weak in the knees and had to take a seat on the bottom step. Within seconds, she passed out from the pain and hysterical crying.

SK had never felt this type of pain in his life. Not even when his blood brother was killed did he feel this way. Bishop was his boy, his right-hand man, and the only person he trusted with his life. This was the same person who actually saved his life on several occasions. This was the only male outside his immediate family he had love for. Now he was gone.

Sarita couldn't stop thinking about what she'd done to Chuck, and if it weren't for a car honking its horn, she probably would have caused an accident. Her phone vibrating in the center console got her attention, and just to be on the safe side, she pulled over to answer it.

"Look at the big-time college man finally finding some time to call his girlfriend!" she answered after seeing his number.

"Don't be like that, bae. I been real busy with the camp. You know I was going to hit you up."

"Yeah, whatever!"

"So what are you doing, smart-ass?"

"Nothing. I'm on my way to Hassan's hearing at the courthouse."

"Oh, you supporting him now?" Nasir asked in a sarcastic way.

"No. I'm going for you since you can't be there. Besides, ya mom asked me to come. She wants to make a day of it, you know, lunch, getting our nails done . . ."

Just hearing her voice did something to Nasir. He badly wanted to see her. "So when are you coming out here? It's nice down South, and this college is crazy."

Up until now Sarita had forgotten about her plans to attend North Carolina with Nasir. So much had been going on that it honestly slipped her mind. "I don't know. I'm hoping to be down there before the summer is out though," she lied. At this time, she wasn't thinking about going to college. She'd just bought a condo and had money to spare, not to mention that she was on the brink of being the largest female heroin distributer in the city of Philly. Millions of dollars were at stake, so when it came down to getting her education or being rich, it was a no-brainer to her. "Bae, I gotta get out of here. This traffic is a mess," she said because she wanted to end the call. "Call me back this evening sometime. I know I'll be free then," she told him. "Love you!"

"I love you too. And tell my mom to take it easy on you at lunch," Nasir chuckled before ending the call.

"Sarita! Sarita!" Isis waved when Sarita walked into the Criminal Justice Center.

It kind of caught Sarita off guard because she hadn't heard from her cousin for a couple of weeks. Isis's aura had changed, too. She went from being a loudmouthed bully to being more humble. She even leaned in and gave Sarita a hug, which was also shocking.

"So how have you been?" Isis asked and pushed the button for the elevator. "But wait! Before you say anything, I really have to apologize for everything I did to you. I was so—"

"You don't have to explain, Isis," Sarita said, cutting her off. "You were never the problem." Sarita's issue was always with Camille. She knew that everything that happened in that house while growing up came from Camille's lack of parenting skills. Isis was just a kid too, following who she thought was the adult in the house. In fact, Sarita remembered more of the good times she had with Isis than the bad.

When they got off the elevator and entered the courtroom, the proceedings had already begun. Camille was already on the stand, and the DA was questioning her about the events that had taken place.

"And as a result of the rape, you said, you became pregnant, right?" the DA asked.

Dion jumped up. "Objection, Your Honor!"

"On what grounds?"

"This is a suppression hearing to see whether the DNA taken from my client was legal. This is not a trial," Dion replied. She was a monster with the law. But even the best lawyers got blindsided every so often. The young female DA came to play ball today.

"Your Honor, the State has another way it would like to establish the legality of the DNA. If I may continue . . ."

The judge overruled Dion's objection and let the DA continue. "Go ahead, Ms. Scott. You can answer the question."

Camille looked to the back of the courtroom at Sarita and Isis sitting to the side. Sarita shook her head, wanting to tell Camille not to reveal who she was.

"As the result of the rape, I was pregnant and had a little girl."

Several side conversations broke out in the courtroom, causing the judge to call for order. Sarita got up and left the courtroom before Camille got a chance to expose her. Dion was also in shock, looking over at Hassan, who had a stupid look on his face. Even the judge had to make sure that what he'd heard was correct. "Ms. Scott, you say that it is your testimony here that you conceived and gave birth to a little girl? Is that correct?"

"Yes, Your Honor," Camille answered while looking over at Hassan.

"Well, is the child available for a DNA test?" the judge inquired.

Camille looked to the back of the courtroom to where Sarita once sat. This prompted everyone in the courtroom to turn around as well. Isis was the only one sitting there, shrugging her shoulders with a confused look on her face.

"I'm sorry, Your Honor, but before I subject my child to something like this, I'm gonna need to talk to her about it," Camille said.

The judge couldn't do anything but respect her wishes. Something like this couldn't just happen overnight. He called for a quick recess, and within minutes he returned and took a seat on the bench. "All right, it is the court's finding that if the DNA of Mr. Johnson is proven through the child's DNA, I'll permit it as evidence. I'm also giving Ms. Scott another thirty days to have a conversation with her daughter. This court cannot and will not force the child to submit her DNA. That is something she will have to do on her own," the judge concluded.

Before the gavel hit the wood, Camille was heading out of the courtroom with Isis right behind her. Hassan wanted to question Camille about the possibility of him having a child, but by the time he got out of the courtroom, she was gone.

Chapter 17

Hassan sat at the kitchen table eating a bowl of cereal when Dion walked in and grabbed a bottle of orange juice from the refrigerator. She walked out without saying a word or even looking Hassan's way. The awkward silence had been going on like this ever since the court hearing where they found out that Hassan could possibly have a child out there. Every time he tried to have a conversation with Dion, she acted like she wasn't paying him any mind.

"Yo, I get it," he said to her when he walked into the bedroom.

Dion was sitting on the bed going over a brief.

"You don't believe me. You think I raped that girl."

Dion just sat there quietly, and her silence became her answer.

Hassan had enough. He left the room only to return with a DVD case in his hand. He walked over to the TV and popped in a disc. "You wanna know some truth?" She acted like she wasn't interested, which made him more upset. "Dion! Dion!" he yelled.

She lifted her head and looked over at the TV, and on the screen was a homemade video. It was of Hassan, Chuck, and two females partying at somebody's house. They were smoking weed, dancing to the music, and swimming in the pool. It took a few minutes, but she recognized one of the females. It was Camille. She was standing over Hassan, flirting with, kissing, and touching him. "What is this?" Dion asked.

"Just shut up and watch it!" Hassan shot back with an obvious attitude.

The screen went blank, then came back on. The scenery had changed from the swimming pool area to the bedroom. Hassan was sitting on the edge of the bed and facing the camera. "I'm about to show you how to lay that pipe," he said, and strategically hid the camera before Camille entered the room. She walked out of the bathroom with only a towel wrapped around her, unaware that she was being filmed.

After sucking his dick for about fifteen minutes, Hassan fucked her every which way. Not only was it consensual, but Camille begged for him to go harder.

"Okay, I've seen enough!" Dion said before she jumped up off the bed and walked over to the TV.

Hassan stopped her before she could turn the DVD off. "After all this shit you putting me through about this rape shit, I swear, Dion, you better watch the whole fuckin' DVD!" he snapped while standing in front of her so she couldn't turn off the TV.

She could see the seriousness in his eyes and hear the conviction in his tone. He was right. Things hadn't been the same since the last court hearing, and she just couldn't shake the possibility of the rape allegations being true. If this was the only way Hassan had to prove his innocence, then she felt like she at least owed it to him to see the footage through. She took a seat back on the bed and watched.

***

Sarita put her surgical mask on and made sure her latex gloves didn't have any defects in them. Shay did the same. Today they were getting their first lesson on how to cut heroin. This was ordered by Hassan because Sarita was going to be handling the product.

Bugsy and Tina were the instructors for the day, and they were going to make sure the girls got it from all angles. By the end of the day, Shay and Sarita were going to know everything about cutting heroin, and it was going to be done within the limits of one kilo. This was probably the most intricate part of the dope game, and once Sarita had it, the sky would be the limit for her.

After Dion collected her thoughts, she went downstairs to talk to Hassan. He was sitting on the living room couch sipping a scotch on the rocks. "You have to let me take this to the DA," she said.

Hassan turned and looked at her like she was crazy. "You can forget about that. The only reason I showed you was so you would get those nut-ass foul thoughts you had of me out of ya mind. That's it and that's all."

"But I can get the charges dropped before the day is out."

"Did you lose ya mind? Did you look at the fuckin' tape, Dion? My kid brother got the smoking gun in his hand!" he snapped.

Chuck was a pain in the ass, but Hassan couldn't bear to throw him under the bus in order to clear his name, not even on a rape charge. And if anybody knew Hassan's heart, it was Dion. She knew that once he had his mind made up, there was nothing that could change it. He was going to stand on that until he was in his grave.

"Baby, I'm sorry," Dion said. She felt like shit, think-ing about all the messed-up things she did to him behind the rape allegations. She had secretly stashed some money away, had sex with his kid brother, and commit-ted the worst evil, which was to hold back a portion of her love. It was a part of her that he never got to experience, and it was unfortunate that she wasn't able to do so. It seemed like everything was about to come to a head, and she felt like time wasn't on her side. The possibility of a rape conviction was possible, Sarita was in possession of pictures of her and Chuck having an affair, and now this. All of this spelled the worst possible outcome.

But Dion wasn't going to sit around and do nothing about it. She was going to try her best to make things right, and the first thing she planned to do was keep Hassan out of jail.

SK looked over and saw that Camille was asleep. She had been for the past hour. Quietly he climbed out of bed and headed out of the room toward the bathroom. He knew he didn't have long before she rolled over and felt that he wasn't there. He went straight to her phone book, and just as he'd hoped, Sarita's name and number were in her phone. He now stored them in his own phone. "Yeah, I got ya ass now!" he mumbled to himself as he walked back to the bedroom.

He couldn't find Hassan to save his life, and Sarita was probably the only person who knew where he was. Camille had tried to get it out of her, but she always came up empty. SK had another way of getting Sarita to talk, one that was sure to have the effect he was looking for. No matter who got hurt, even if Camille knew her, he was going to find Hassan. And as far as he was concerned, Sarita had something to do with Bishop's death, especially since she knew where the body was.

SK climbed back into the bed and placed Camille's phone back on the nightstand. He looked at her and almost regretted the way things were about to unravel. He had come to like her, but at the end of the day, she might be the one to get the bad end of the stick.

The entire process of cutting and weighing the heroin literally took half the day. Sarita and Shay didn't come up for air until four o'clock in the afternoon.

"Take in as much fresh air as you can," Tina said, coming out onto the porch with Sarita and Shay. "If you're not careful, that shit can get into your system, and the next thing you know, you'll be using the product instead of selling it."

Shay took in deeper breaths after hearing that. She saw firsthand what heroin could do to people. After Tina went back into the house, Shay and Sarita stayed outside.

"What're you over there thinking about?" Shay asked.

Sarita was staring across the street at an empty lot. She had a lot on her mind, and most important was her decision whether to let Hassan live or die. She had pretty much done everything she set out to do thus far. She managed to rob him for a half million dollars, muscle her way into his organization, and was in possession of $5 million worth of heroin. She also had Torres on board with the takeover, had most of the workers in the organization loyal to her, and was on the verge of ruining Hassan's marriage with the pictures of Chuck and Dion. And if she wanted to, she could have put him in prison for the rest of his life, or at least for a very long time, not to mention that she'd killed Chuck, Hassan's brother. At this point she could afford to let him live and not have to worry about any repercussions.

On the other hand, her heart was telling her to finish what she had started. She had come this far and thought about the totality of the circumstances.

Here was a man who had raped her mother and gotten away with it, which was why she had endured all the pain and torture she'd been through over the years. No amount of money could make her forget or forgive Hassan for that. It was all because of him, and after taking all of this into consideration, she came to the conclusion that it was time for her to end this chapter of her life. And the only way she was going to do that was to take Hassan's life.

"Remember when I told you that I was going to kill the man who raped my mom?" she asked Shay.

"Yeah, I remember. And whatever you need me to do, I'm wit' you," Shay said, not hesitating to assist.

Killing Hassan was going to be easy, but Sarita wanted to make sure that she got away with it. It had to be at the right time, in the right place, and under the right circumstances, and nothing could come back to her. There was going to be a life after this, and the last thing she wanted was to be in prison or die because she had been sloppy in committing the crime.

"Oh, this must be important if you had to come all the way out here," Bob said when Dion walked into his office. Bob was the firm's private investigator, but he also had his own business. "So what can I do for you?" he asked. "Something to do with the Scott case?"

Dion had been trying all day but couldn't come up with anything pertaining to Camille's history. There were no hospital records of her giving birth in Pennsylvania, nor were there any school records that could lead back to her. The child she claimed she had was like a ghost and a lie. That would go well in court when she attacked Camille's credibility, but before that could happen, she needed to be sure of it. "Bob, what I'm asking of you is to stay between us," she said, taking a seat in the chair in front of his desk.

"Aha! Now this should be good," Bob replied, rubbing his hands together.

"I need you to find somebody for me. This woman claims to have had a kid, but there's no record of it," Dion said, passing Bob the folder with Camille's info in it. "If she has a child, I need you to inform me of her whereabouts as soon as possible. But on the other hand, if you find that she doesn't have any kids, I need you to give me concrete evidence of that as well." She reached in her bag and pulled out a wad of money and passed it to Bob. "This is five grand. I need you to get on top of this like it's priority one."

Five grand was overpayment for a small job like this, so Bob was more than willing to jump all over it. Finding people was his specialty, and if a female gave birth to any child within the United States, he could find out about it. "Give me forty-eight hours, and I'll have something for you," he assured her.

With no pass to go outside today, Hassan walked around the house trying to find something to do. He grabbed his phone and tried to call Chuck, thinking this could be a good time for them to talk and clear the air on a couple of issues. He specifically wanted to talk about the business and what the future may hold for them. "Come on, li'l nigga. Answer the phone," he mumbled to himself as he stepped outside to get some fresh air.

Chuck's phone went to voicemail after a couple of rings. "Yo, bro, I know you might still be mad at me, but hit me back when you get this," Hassan said to the voicemail.

Hassan looked around and was bored as hell. He looked at the lawn and the Cadillac Escalade that was in the driveway. It was either going to be cutting grass or washing the cars. It was ninety degrees outside today, and washing the cars seemed like the better option. He went back into the house, changed clothes, and grabbed the car-washing supplies. The Cadillac truck was the dirtiest, so that was where he started.

"Hey, Hassan!" a voice called. It was Shelly, a middle-aged white woman who lived across the street. She always pulled out a chair when he decided to wash his car with only a pair of shorts on.

Hassan began spraying the truck down with the hose, and when he got to the back, the color of the water streaming down the back door was red. He turned the hose away so he could get a better look. "What da hell is this?" he mumbled and sprayed the back door again to wash the red streams away. He then looked closer at the door, and to his surprise there was what seemed to be a bullet hole. Smudges were all over the windows as well, which caught his attention too. He grabbed the rag out of the bucket and wiped it across the window. A light coat of blood covered the rag. "What da fuck!" he said with his face twisted up.

He reached into his pocket and grabbed his phone to call Sarita. She and Chuck were the last people with the truck, and if something happened without either of them saying anything, there was going to be a problem.

"Yeah?" Sarita answered as she was leaving the trap house.

"I'm sitting out here washing the Cadillac, and it looks like you had a little fender bender. I need you to make your way over here so we can talk about it," Hassan said, then hung up the phone before she could say anything.

To avoid being in possession of evidence that may be linked to a crime, Hassan finished washing the truck, took a pair of pliers, and removed the bullet from the back door.

Sarita looked up at the sky and then let out a frustrated sigh. She really didn't want to deal with Hassan right now. Making sure that the product was hitting the streets was her priority. "Tina! I'll be right back!" she yelled into the house.

Sarita didn't make it off the steps before two black SUVs sped down the street from both directions. She knew that it had to be the cops, and it was only out of fear that she didn't run back into the house to warn Tina and Bugsy. Before she knew it, several armed men jumped out of the SUVs. They didn't look like the cops, and it wasn't until she felt the thump on the side of her head that she realized they weren't cops. She dropped to her knees, holding the side of her head, and when Bugsy tried to exit the house, SK fired a single shot at him, causing him to retreat.

"Where da fuck is Hassan!" SK yelled while standing over Sarita.

Sarita was still in shock and thought she felt blood dripping down the side of her head. "I don't know. I don't know where he lives," she answered, trying to get to her feet.

The confrontation was starting to get the attention of some of the neighbors on the block.

"Bitch, you coming wit' us!" he said, and cracked her on the head with his gun.

A black sack was thrown over her head, and she was thrown into one of the SUVs.

SK took one last look up and down the street before he got into the car and pulled off. Just as fast as they pulled up to the block, the SUVs pulled off.

Tina ran out of the house with a Mossberg pump, but she didn't fire a shot because she wasn't sure which SUV Sarita was in.

Chapter 18

Camille could feel something was wrong from the moment she woke up that morning. SK hadn't come in last night, and when she looked at her phone on the nightstand, she saw that she didn't have any missed calls or text messages. That was also unusual. Calling SK's cell came up short, too, because his phone went straight to voicemail. Now she was starting to become worried. "Where in the hell are you?" she mumbled to herself, looking down at her phone.

She made another call, but this time she called the club, and surprisingly, SK answered his office phone. "Club Vanity!" he answered.

"Hey, babe, I was starting to get a little worried. Is everything good?" she asked, getting out of the bed.

Her voice caught SK off guard, and had he taken the time to check the caller ID, he would not have answered. "Yeah, yeah. Everything is good. Something came up last night. I meant to call you and tell you. My bad." He looked over at his boy Rock, who was sitting on the couch and shaking his head.

"So do you need me to stop by and help you out with anything?"

"Nah, babe. I'm gonna be tied up for the rest of the day. I'll see you tonight."

"You don't want any lunch or an extra shot of me?" she asked in a seductive manner.

"As good as that sounds, I have to turn you down. But how about you go into the top drawer and grab a couple of grand and do some shopping? And I'll try to get out of here early so we can get dinner," SK told her.

Something didn't seem right. His tone of voice seemed somewhat dismissive. It was like he wanted to keep her away from the club. But she didn't make a fuss, especially since she could do some shopping today. "Okay, babe. Call me back when you're free." She ended the call.

"Yo, I think we should start pressing the issue of this takeover," Rock said, lying out flat on the couch. "The streets are talking, but not about us. Da nigga Hassan holds too much weight, and he's not even in the game right now, my nigga. How crazy is that?"

"Yeah. And that li'l bitch can take a punch, too!" SK said, referring to Sarita, whom he had tied up in the basement of the club. All he wanted to know was where Hassan rested his head, but she refused to say anything.

"So what do you want me to do wit' shorty downstairs?" Rock asked, not having any tolerance or patience.

"Nah, she's gonna tell me what I want to know. Let her ass stay down there with the mice and rats for a couple of days. In the meantime, start advancing on Jefferson Street, Ithan Street, and Catherine Street. Put the press on them niggas and give them the *State Property* offer," SK said.

This confused Rock. "And what in the hell is the *State Property* offer?" he asked.

"'You either get down or lay down. And if you lay down, you stay down,'" SK said, quoting Beanie Sigel.

Rock was feeling that line and repeated it just to see how it would sound coming out of his mouth. SK chuckled, then turned and focused on his computer screen. He didn't need to check on Sarita right now. Now that he had her, he was going to take his time.

Hassan stood in Chuck's living room, and at one point he had to cover his nose because of the strong stench of rotten chicken and other foods that were laid out on the counter. The condo looked deserted. Dust had accumulated on the coffee table in the living room, dirty dishes were in the sink, Chuck's bedroom had clothes all over the place, and the AC wasn't on, so it was hot and muggy throughout the whole condo.

Hassan pulled out his phone and tried to call Chuck, but the call went straight to voicemail. This wasn't like Chuck, not even if he was mad at Hassan.

He didn't attempt to call Chuck back but instead tried to call Sarita. She was supposed to stop by the house the other day to explain the bullet hole and the blood on the Cadillac, but she never showed up. "You gotta be kidding me!" Hassan said when he didn't get an answer.

His gut was telling him that something was wrong, but he only had a couple more hours to be outside on his day pass. He was supposed to go and see Dion at the law office, but that was a no go. All he wanted to do at this point was check up on his people.

The gag in Sarita's mouth made it hard for her to swallow. Her throat was bone dry, and she could feel the rag piercing the skin at the corners of her mouth. Her wrists and ankles were bound with zip ties that were so tight they made her bleed. She couldn't get up if she wanted to, and even if she could, she wouldn't get anywhere. SK had her locked inside of an old cooler they didn't use. The temperature in the cooler was in the nineties, and there were times when she had to scare mice away.

Please, God, help me! she silently prayed as tears fell from her eyes. She tried to scream, but the sound was muffled by the gag. She heard someone coming down the stairs and said another silent prayer. A set of keys jangled before the door of the cooler opened.

He was far from God, but SK did have Sarita's life in his hands. He walked in, pulled up a chair, and sat next to her. "It's hot as hell! down here," he said, pulling out his lighter to light his blunt. "You wanna know the fucked-up part about it? Hassan is probably home right now with his feet up, drinking a glass of lemonade." He took a pull of the weed.

Sarita tried to say something through the gag, so SK reached over and pulled it out of her mouth. "Please! I'll give you whatever you want!" she pleaded.

"I'm not tryin'a hear that shit. You gon' tell me what I want to know or I'ma leave ya ass down here to die. The muthafuckin' rats are gonna have a field day eating at you."

Sarita began to cry just thinking about it.

"Now, I'ma ask you something, and you better tell me the truth," SK warned. "Did you have anything to do with killing Bishop?"

"No! I swear he was already dead when I got to the house!"

"Don't fuckin' lie to me! How da fuck did you know where his body was?" SK yelled.

Sarita knew, but she couldn't tell him the whole truth. SK would more than likely kill her on the spot if she confessed to helping Chuck get rid of the body in Cobbs Creek. "I know because I overheard Hassan telling someone else about it. That's why I couldn't give Camille specifics on where the body was. Now can you please let me go?" she pleaded.

SK wasn't done yet. "Where did he change his house arrest to? And don't play stupid, because I know you know."

Sarita lay there thinking about whether she should tell him. But if she did, she knew that afterward he wouldn't have any use for her. She definitely couldn't see him letting her go out of the kindness of his heart. Self-preservation became her number one priority. "If you let me go, I'll give you two and a half million dollars' worth of heroin. That's fifty kilos, uncut," she offered.

"Bitch, stop lying!" SK said, and flicked the ashes of his blunt onto her head.

"I'm not lying. I got access to it right now."

"That's Hassan's dope?"

"If it really matters to you, yes, it's his dope."

SK took another pull of the weed and blew the smoke in Sarita's face. "Tell me where it's at."

Sarita looked up at him like he was crazy. "Don't insult me," she replied, and lowered her head. She could tell that the amount of dope she offered had gotten his attention. "You must think I'm a damn fool," she chuckled.

"A'ight, you got a deal," he lied, and turned his head away.

"Fuck you! Let me go and I'll give you the dope. If not, then you might as well kill me right now, 'cause I'm not giving you shit until I'm free," Sarita said with conviction.

SK took another pull of the weed and blew the smoke in her face again. $2.5 million in heroin was a lot of product and a lot of money once he put it out on the streets.

SK was thirsty for money, and even though he didn't want to show it, Sarita could see it. At that moment, she felt she had enough leverage to live another day, along with a little more control over the situation. "Now go back upstairs and renegotiate my release," she told him with a hint of confidence.

SK reached down, grabbed the gag, and stuffed it back into her mouth. A stiff kick to the gut was what she got before he walked out of the cooler.

Workers were shocked to see Hassan when he pulled up to the block. He hadn't made rounds in weeks, and some were thinking that he was out of the game.

"Shit! The last time I saw him was a couple nights ago," one of the workers told Hassan when he asked if he'd seen Chuck around.

Every answer from every worker sounded the same. Nobody had seen Chuck for a couple of days, which was around the same night he and Sarita made the pickup. Even more surprising was that the product wasn't getting to the workers. It was like the entire operation had come to a stop. Because of that, Hassan knew for sure that something was going on.

Even though SK told her not to, Camille still showed up to the club. It was out of curiosity more than anything else. She just knew that when she walked through the doors, SK would be there doing something he had no business doing. During the drive there, she'd prepared herself for it.

When she walked up and tried to open the double glass doors, they were locked. "I know somebody's in here," she said to herself, cupping her hands together to look through the window.

Rock was on his way upstairs when he glanced over and saw her at the door. "Damn!" he mumbled and walked over to the doors to let her in. "I thought you was still out shopping," he joked, stepping to the side.

"Surprise, surprise!" she laughed and headed upstairs to SK's office. She felt a little bad when she opened the office door and saw him sitting behind the desk with his face in the computer. No females were in sight.

"I thought I told you that I was going to be busy all day."

"I know, boo, but I was missing you," Camille said, looking around the office.

SK chuckled as he watched her looking for a female. He then refocused his attention on the computer.

"A'ight, I get the picture. What time will you be coming in tonight?"

SK sat there thinking for a moment. He had Sarita in the basement, and he knew for sure that she was going to be upset. But he really didn't have any other choice at the time. "Yo, I need ya help on something, but I don't want you to get mad."

"Why would I be mad?"

"I know for sure you're gonna be mad, but I need you. You said you was gonna ride wit' me through whatever, right?"

"Yeah, yeah, I hear you. Spit it out."

"You gotta promise me that you won't get mad first. And remember, your word is everything."

Camille thought about it for a moment. It probably wasn't as bad as she thought. "A'ight, I promise, bae. Just get on with it."

SK got up from behind his desk, walked over and grabbed Camille's hand, and led her out of the office.

"Where are we going?" she asked as they headed for the basement. "A quickie? I likey-likey!" She smiled.

"Nah, no quickie. But if you can close the deal on this one, I'm sure you'll bust a nut with the amount of money that's involved. Now don't freak out," he said, walking her up to the cooler door. When he opened it, Sarita was still lying there where he left her.

Camille looked down at Sarita's bruised and bloody face and almost had twins on the spot. Sarita looked up and couldn't believe who was standing over her.

"What da fuck, SK! You lost ya mind?" Camille snapped. "Get her the fuck out of here!" she continued and reached down in an attempt to remove the zip ties from Sarita's wrists and ankles.

"Hold the fuck up! Dis li'l bitch ain't goin' nowhere! I told you I was going to find Hassan no matter what!" SK yelled back. "Now if you on some other shit, let me know!" He pulled Camille out of the cooler seeing that she was upset. But he didn't know how upset she was.

Had Camille been packing, she would have shot him in the face by now. "Let me ask you this: what da fuck do you want me to do?" she asked with obvious anger in her tone.

"All I need you to do is get her to tell you where Hassan lives, and that's it."

"And that's it? What about her? You gon' let her go after she tells you?"

SK looked away. It looked like he was thinking about it, but in all actuality he wasn't. His mind was already made up from the moment he took Sarita. He was going to put a bullet in her head as well. "Yeah, I'll let her go," he lied.

Camille could see right through him though, and she had to play along. She didn't want him to think that she wasn't riding with him, because there was a strong possibility that she could catch a bullet right along with Sarita and Hassan. "I'll talk to her, but let me do it myself," she requested.

SK walked over and looked through the small window on the door. Sarita wasn't in any shape to try to do anything, let alone try to pull off an escape. "Do it!"

Hassan pulled into his driveway and was tempted to reverse and pull back out. Being on house arrest was in the way, and it ate at him how he couldn't get anything done in that short period of time that was allotted to him by the judge. So much needed to be done.

Hassan didn't even get a chance to talk to Sarita about the night she and Chuck went to pick up the shipment. From all the information he gathered today concerning the whereabouts of Chuck, the blood on the Cadillac door, and the bullet that was lodged in the back door, he was coming to the strong conclusion that Chuck might be dead. It wasn't as if he would have any mercy on Sarita if he found out that she was behind his demise, but the most important thing was to find out what happened. After that, and if she did have anything to do with it, he was going to kill her in the worst way.

Camille walked back into the office, where SK was looking as normal as he could considering she was under the impression that he had Sarita hogtied and beaten.

"Did you put the gag back in her mouth?" he asked, looking up from the computer screen.

"Of course. And she's willing to give me five million dollars in dope as well," Camille said as she stood in front of the desk.

SK's eyes shot open like two fifty-cent pieces. "Five million?" he asked, getting up from the desk. "Damn! How did you pull that off?"

"She's got access to almost a hundred kilos."

"That li'l lying bitch!" SK shot back.

"You gotta know how to say the right things. Plus, I gave her my word that we were going to let her go. She was certain that you were going to kill her," Camille said, wrapping her arms around his waist. "We'll do it tonight. She has to make a few phone calls to gather everything up."

As Camille spoke, her eyes couldn't stop looking around the room to find something to bash him in the head with. The only thing that stopped her from doing so was the fact that he had numerous men all over the club, all of whom were armed. It was that, and because she wanted to give him a way out. She wanted to give him the chance to do the right thing. She owed him that much after the relationship they'd built.

Chapter 19

On her way home from work, Dion got a call from Bob explaining that he had found something. It was a no-brainer that Dion shot right over to his office.

When she pulled up to the building, her heart began to race for reasons she couldn't understand. Was it the possibility that Camille wasn't lying about having a kid, or even worse, that the kid was Hassan's? These thoughts and more raced through her head as she raced down the hallway to Bob's office.

"I'm glad you could make it," Bob said, getting up from his desk to shake her hand.

"Give it to me straight, Bob," Dion replied.

Bob tapped the keys on his laptop, and then turned the screen around so Dion could see what he was looking at.

It appeared that Camille did have a child, and her name was Sarita. At least, that was what the school records showed. Dion didn't think to check the local school records, but there it was in black and white. The records were from over eight years ago, and they indicated that Camille was the mother of the 8-year-old girl.

"I know you told me to give it to you straight, but I have to warn you that what I'm about to show you might be a little disturbing," Bob warned. He reached over and grabbed the laptop from Dion, tapped at the keys again, and then turned it back around to her. "I don't think your husband has been completely honest with you."

The first picture that popped up was a photo of Hassan and Sarita at the gas station together. Dion kept scrolling down, and there were pictures of Sarita driving Hassan's Range Rover and entering and leaving the house. There were also pictures of Sarita sitting alone while on her phone in the restaurant Dion and Hassan owned. "Is this the girl you're talking about?" Dion asked with a confused look on her face.

"Yup! That's Sarita Powell, all eighteen years of her," Bob answered, sitting back in his chair. "I almost could have gotten her DNA, but she threw the empty water bottle into the car she was driving instead of the trash. But hell, being honest, the girl looks like ya husband."

Dion looked at Sarita's picture, and then looked at Hassan's, and up until now she never really knew how much Sarita looked like Hassan. His dark eyelashes, the way their ears were pointed at the top, the one deep dimple on the left side of their cheeks . . . If Dion had to make a guess, she would think that Sarita was his. That in itself could potentially become a problem for Hassan in court. With Camille's testimony and a positive DNA test, he was sure to be found guilty. Dion only hoped that he would give up the only evidence that could free him from this case.

Hassan stared up into the clear night sky. He was standing on his back deck trying to clear his head. He wondered about Chuck, Sarita, court, and where the hell his dope was. His phone ringing on the table snapped him out of his thoughts. Not recognizing the number, he answered anyway. "Yo!"

"Darnell, please don't hang up," Camille said.

"What do you want?" he barked when he heard her voice.

"Sarita was kidnapped, and I know where she's at."

That really got his attention. "What do you mean? As a matter of fact, where are you?"

Camille beeped the horn twice. "I'm outside."

Hassan darted into the house and grabbed his gun from the dining room table. For Camille to know where he lived was a breach in security, and he didn't know what to expect. He peeked through the blinds and saw Camille get out of her car. She looked like she was alone, but that didn't make him rest any easier. When she got up to the door, he flung it open and pointed the gun at her head. He looked around suspiciously and waited for someone to jump out of the bushes.

"I'm by myself," Camille said.

Hassan patted her down. He took the gun from her waistband, then let her in.

"My ex-boyfriend kidnapped Sarita, and now he wants two and a half million dollars for her," Camille said.

"Who da fuck is ya ex-boyfriend?" Hassan pointed the gun in her direction.

Camille was hesitant to answer. She took a deep breath. "SK." She exhaled.

Hassan's face tightened. "The fuck? How you gonna date that nigga?"

"I ain't gonna get into that. I'm here to get help for Sarita. He's torturing her. She somehow has two and a half million dollars in dope, and he wants it." She wiped tears from her cheek. "I'm supposed to be checking on the dope, but I know as soon as I confirm that I got it, he's gonna kill her."

"Sarita told you where the dope was at?" Hassan asked.

"Yeah, she told me, but I'm not telling you unless you go and get her."

"Go and get who? Sarita? Why da fuck should I go and get her? She told the muthafucka where my dope was."

"Because she's ya daughter!" Camille replied, lowering her head in humility.

Hassan lowered his gun and asked, "What did you just say?" He wanted to be clear on what he'd heard.

"I said Sarita is ya daughter, Darnell. And I know. I'm sorry—"

"Shut up! Shut da fuck up!" he yelled, now pointing the gun back at her. "You're lying! You're lying because that's what you do, just like you're trying to put me in prison!"

"I promise you that you won't do a day in prison. I'm gonna make it right. Just go and get our daughter back." Camille's motherly instinct had kicked in over the past few weeks, and she realized the way she carried the whole situation with Sarita was wrong. When she walked in and saw Sarita tied up and lying on the floor, she knew at that moment it was time for her to act like a mother, even if it was for this one time.

"I know one thing. You better not be lying," Hassan said. He didn't want to believe Camille, but he felt she was telling the truth. He couldn't live with himself if he stood by and let his daughter get murdered. Then there was the possibility of his court issues going away and that he wanted his heroin back. "Tell me where she's at."

SK snapped his fingers at his boys to tell them to be quiet so he could answer the phone. He hoped this was the call he'd been waiting for.

"It's here, so send as many people as you can," Camille said when SK answered his phone.

SK smiled. The unexpected score was about to put him on top of the game for real.

"Oh, and that address for Hassan checked out, too. He's home alone right now," Camille added.

SK hung up the phone. Everything was coming to a head, and it was time to close it out. "Yo, load up!" He got up from his desk. He gave his boys the location. "Make sure you niggas be on point at all times, and bring my dope here."

"Damn, bro! I thought you was coming with us," Rock said.

"Nah, I got some unfinished business to take care of." SK cocked a bullet into the chamber of his .40-cal.

"What about da li'l bitch downstairs? You want me to kill her?"

Before Camille left the club, she got SK to agree that they wouldn't kill Sarita until Hassan was dead. She convinced them that as long as Sarita was alive, they would always have a piece of insurance in the event that Hassan slipped through the cracks. SK didn't just think that it was a good idea, he thought it was genius. "Nah, I'll take care of that later. Just get my dope."

While Hassan dipped in and out of traffic, he knew that a window of opportunity had just opened up. According to Camille, the bulk of the threat at the club was now on the way to retrieve the dope. But Hassan honestly couldn't care less about who was there. His entire frame of mind had changed, and this had become a mission to save his daughter. Thinking about the possibility of being a father was overwhelming. Just thinking about her made him smile, and he began to see many of his characteristics in her. "Damn, Sarita! Why didn't you say anything?" he mumbled as he was pulling off the highway. The way he was feeling right now was crazy. He was so excited about fatherhood that he put the incident with Chuck on the back burner.

Then thoughts of him forgiving Sarita invaded his thoughts, something he couldn't understand at the moment. He didn't know that the bond between a father and his daughter was strong, but he was finding out with every minute that passed. "Hold on, baby girl! I'm coming!" Hassan mumbled again as he pulled up to the side of the club. "Daddy's here!"

Dion walked into the house and threw her bag on the couch. "Hassan!" she called out while going up the steps. "Babe, you're not gonna believe this shit!" She walked into the bedroom and looked around. Hassan was nowhere in sight. "Babe!" she called out again before running back downstairs with haste.

"He's not here," a female voice said from the darkest part of the room. This startled Dion. Camille came out of the shadows with a gun in her hand.

"Oh, bitch, you must'a bumped ya head coming up in my house!" Dion snapped, walking toward Camille in attack mode.

Camille quickly raised the gun to make Dion slow down, but it was as if Dion didn't see it, or she didn't care.

Wop!

Dion punched Camille so hard she knocked her onto the couch. It dazed her long enough for Dion to grab the gun in Camille's hand. She tried to take it, but Camille wouldn't let it go. She really didn't want to shoot Dion, but she might be left with no other choice. Camille could only imagine what Dion would do if she got hold of the gun.

Dion was relentless, too, rearing back and punching Camille several more times in the face. Her grip was getting weaker, and right at the very moment when Camille was about to fire off a shot, Dion stopped. She froze when she felt the barrel of a gun being pressed on the back of her head. Camille looked up, and standing there behind Dion was SK. Neither one of them heard him creep in.

"Where da fuck is he?" SK asked in a low voice just in case Hassan was in the house.

Camille jumped up from the chair and stood next to SK. Dion turned around, looking down the barrel of the gun.

"He's not here. He left a few minutes ago," Camille said, wiping the blood from the corner of her mouth. She clutched the gun tightly while taking the safety off.

Dion just stood there. She was scared to death knowing she was about to be shot. The empty look in SK's eyes told her so.

"Give ya husband this message for me."

Before he could get the shot off, Camille put her gun to the back of his head. SK twisted his face up in utter disbelief. "What da fuck are you doing?" he snapped, turning around to face her.

Camille took a step back, putting space between the two. She gave SK more than enough chances to do the right thing by letting Sarita go, but his heart was set on killing her and Hassan and anybody who got in the way. Though it had been years since she showed any type of love toward Sarita, she was her daughter, and she wasn't about to let anybody kill her, especially not SK. "I'm sorry!" she said, looking into SK's eyes.

He lunged forward in an attempt to grab the gun, but he was too late. Camille squeezed the trigger, sending a hot lead ball into his face. The bullet hit him over his left eye. He fell to the ground right by her feet and rolled over onto his back.

Dion just stood there in shock, not believing what she'd just witnessed. Her being next was the only thing that went through her mind. When Camille turned and pointed the gun at her, she knew she was dead.

"He came here to kill you and ya husband, and then he was going to kill my daughter, Sarita," Camille told her.

Dion was about to start begging for her life, but there was no need to at this point.

"So this is how it's gonna work. When the cops get here, you're gonna tell them that he broke into your house and tried to rape you. That's when you shot him," Camille explained.

Dion looked down at the body and then back up at Camille.

"You got it?" Camille yelled.

Dion nodded.

Camille walked over to her and started to pass her the gun, but she didn't let it go right away. She looked Dion in her eyes and said, "You're gonna need some gunpowder on ya hand," she advised as she grabbed her bag off the floor.

Being a lawyer, Dion knew exactly what that meant. As Camille was walking out the door, Dion stood over SK and fired a single shot into his chest.

Pop!

"Watch the front door. If anybody comes out of there besides me or Sarita, shoot 'em," Hassan told Shy, one of his top shooters.

Then he walked around to the back of the club. He checked the door that Camille said would be unlocked. It didn't budge. He pulled it again. No luck. He looked for another way in. He noticed several small windows lining the ground level of the building. Most of them were tinted except for two of them, so Hassan could see it was the basement. "Damn!" He used the butt of his gun to smash the window. He tapped gingerly to try to make the least amount of sound.

Tick! Tick! Tick!

One more tap on the glass and it broke. He looked around to see if anybody had seen him, and when he was sure the coast was clear, he climbed in.

It was relatively dark as he moved through the basement, but he found the broken cooler way off in the back. He looked through the window on the cooler door and saw Sarita tied up inside. He opened the door, and at first it didn't look like she was breathing. But when he knelt down next to her, he saw she was.

He looked at Sarita's wrists and saw they were bound by zip-ties. He strained to rip them off, but they just dug into her skin. He looked around for something to cut Sarita loose. He ran out of the cooler and saw a pair of wire cutters on the floor.

He cut her loose. "Come on, Sarita. You gotta get up," he said, smacking the side of her face. It took a few times, but she came to. She opened her eyes to see Hassan standing over her.

"Sarita, we gotta get out of here. Can you walk?"

She nodded, then staggered to her feet.

Hassan led her back to the window he had come through. "Take this," he said, passing her the gun before she climbed out the window.

Suddenly the lights in the basement came on. Hassan could hear the voices of a couple of men coming down the stairs. He jumped up to pull himself through the window, and as his body was halfway out, Sarita pulled him the rest of the way.

Out of nowhere, she pointed the gun at him when he stood up. He didn't see this coming at all. "Sarita, we don't have time for this," he said in a soft voice.

The entire time she was lying on the ground, tied up and beaten, she thought of a million ways to kill him. She promised herself that if and when the opportunity presented itself, she was going to take it.

"I know who you are," Hassan said, looking into her eyes. "I know you are my daughter."

"Shut up! You don't know shit!" Sarita snapped back. "You're a fuckin' rapist, and I hate you! You don't deserve to live!"

The two men who came down the basement steps could be heard yelling once they saw Sarita wasn't in the cooler.

"Sarita, I don't know what ya mom told you, but I didn't rape her."

"Fuck you!"

"We can't talk about this right now. We gotta get out of here," he said, walking toward her with his hands in the air.

Shooting him right now was a little harder than Sarita thought it would be. Tears filled her eyes.

Hassan got all the way up to her and wrapped his arms around his daughter for the first time. "I got you now. We'll fix it together," he whispered in her ear.

Sarita enjoyed the moment she had with her father, and deep down inside, she wished things could have been different. "I love you, Daddy!" she said, wrapping one arm around him and then jamming the gun into his side.

Pop!

Hassan reared back with a confused look on his face. The bullet crashed through his ribcage and pierced his lung before exiting through his back. He stumbled back up against the wall, holding his side where the bullet hit him. He couldn't get any words out because blood was filling his lungs.

Sarita didn't want to hear anything else from him anyway. She aimed the gun at his chest and fired again.

Pop!

His body slid down the wall. Sarita approached him, and as he appeared to be taking his last breath, she fired another shot at his head to take him out of his misery. "Goodbye, Dad!" she said, then turned and faded into the night.

Camille pulled up to Crescent Point, an apartment complex on the outskirts of the city. Sarita had turned this into her first stash house that only she and a few other people knew about. Hassan wasn't one of them.

Camille took the ten-shot .40-caliber from under the seat before exiting the car. She was a bit nervous about what was waiting for her on the other side of the door. This was where the ninety-nine kilos of heroin were supposed to be. Camille wasn't sure if that was the truth or if this was a plot to have her killed.

Camille cocked a bullet into the chamber before crossing the street and walking up the steps. She kept the gun in her hand while constantly checking her surroundings.

Tina opened the door before Camille could knock. In her hands was a sawed-off shotgun pointed at Camille.

"Sarita called you," Camille said, fearing that she was about to be shot. The gun in her hand was of no use at this point because one blast from the shotgun would end her. Tina stepped back so Camille could enter the house, but the shotgun remained aimed at her.

"Lose the gun!" Tina demanded, which Camille had no problem doing, stuffing it into her back pocket.

Tina already had the dope bagged up and ready to go as instructed by Sarita. "Is she okay?" she asked. "And don't fuckin' lie!"

Camille was shaken. "Yes, she's fine. As soon as I can get out of here and get this dope to where it's supposed to go, she'll be released. I want her back just as much as you do."

Tina didn't know Camille and had never met her before, but she did get a good look at her face. She nodded for Camille to grab the two duffle bags. Camille threw them over her shoulders.

Tina kept the shotgun pointed at her the entire time to the front door. "If she's not released in the next hour, I give you my word, you'll be dead before sunrise," she said, then slammed the door behind her.

Chapter 20

Visions of Hassan's body falling to the ground flashed through Sarita's head. And after driving around the city all night to clear her head, she ended up going home, the only place where she felt comfortable and safe. As soon as she walked through the door, she kicked her shoes off and walked over to the minibar. She grabbed a bottle of Cîroc and headed out to the balcony for some air. "Damn, Sarita! What did you do?" she asked herself before she took a swig from the bottle.

The reality hit her, and though she justified it in her mind, the fact remained that she killed her own father. She didn't know why she was feeling so much regret behind it, but it made her take another swig of the bottle.

She looked out into the night sky and tried to drink her thoughts away. The only thing was that the more she drank, the more she began to think. She thought about all the questions she had for Hassan and what had really happened between him and Camille. She wanted to know the truth, having a few doubts about Camille's version of the story.

Oddly, she wanted to know if she had any honest and caring family members on his side. Did she have a grandmother, grandfather, brothers, sisters, aunts, and uncles she would like to get to know? "Shit! It wasn't their fault my father was a rapist," she said and took another swig of the Cîroc.

Sarita was good and tipsy, and her thoughts were starting to speak a sober tune. "I miss you, Daddy!" She began to cry.

More and more questions arose from her intoxicated mind. There were questions she wanted answers to, but she could no longer get them from the source—Hassan. Visions of his lifeless body hitting the ground were reminders that he wasn't going to be able to tell her anything.

Camille lay in bed and waited for an important phone call from Shooter, who would let her know that SK had been shot and killed. When the call finally came, she answered in a fake groggy voice. "Hello."

Shooter was standing in front of Hassan's house watching the coroner bring out SK's body. "Yo, wake up. SK just got shot," he said, watching the flashing red and blue lights.

Because Camille was such an actor, she changed her tone of voice to one of concern. "Is he all right? Is he all right?" she asked, and then held the phone away from her face so she could light a cigarette.

When Shooter told her that SK was dead, she continued the act by going ballistic and began yelling and pleading for Shooter to tell her where he was.

It was almost two o'clock in the morning when the homicide detectives finished collecting their evidence from Hassan's house and released the body. But Camille didn't care. She was prepared to get her day started with first figuring out how and when she was going to start pushing the dope out into the streets.

"I'll come and get you in like thirty minutes," Shooter told her. "Be ready, 'cause we got a long day ahead of us," he said, then hung up the phone.

Camille didn't even get a chance to put her phone down before it started to ring again. This was another call she was expecting. Within seconds of answering the phone, she could tell that Sarita had been drinking. Her voice was low, and her speech was slurred.

"I did it, Camille. I did it, and I don't even care," Sarita said as she sat on the balcony with a half-full bottle of Cîroc sitting between her legs.

"Sarita, what did you do?" Camille asked, afraid of the answer. "Sarita! Sarita!" she yelled.

"I shot 'im! I killed the muthafucka who raped you!"

Camille's chin hit the ground when she heard that.

"He did rape you, didn't he, Mommy?" Sarita's slurred voice continued.

In Camille's eyes, this was like a blessing in disguise. No more court hearings and her not having to lie anymore was a weight off her shoulders. There would be no more having to worry about retaliation and no more having to lie to Sarita about him. And most importantly, she didn't have to worry about Hassan running half the city. Her takeover plan was in effect.

But before she could celebrate, she had to make sure that Hassan hadn't said anything to Sarita before he died. "Sarita, I need you to listen to me," Camille said, getting out of her bed. "Did Hassan say anything to you? Did y'all talk about anything?"

Sarita was starting to go in and out of consciousness.

"Sarita, did you talk to him?" Camille yelled, trying to wake her up.

"Yeah. He called you a lying bitch, and that's when I shot him." Those were the last words she could get out before she nodded off into a deep sleep.

That was music to Camille's ears. "You did good, baby. Now try to get some sleep, and I'll call you later on," she said, then hung up the phone.

Everything seemed like it was coming together for Camille. The only thing left was for her to walk a mile in Hassan's and SK's shoes and have the entire city eating out of the palm of her hand.

"We've got a pulse again!" the nurse called out to the doctors who were working on Hassan.

Dr. Kemble, who was the top surgeon, was two seconds away from calling the time of death on Hassan for the fourth time. Throughout the night, Hassan died and came back so many times that the nurses could only give the credit to God.

The operating room was chaotic. Nurses and doctors were yelling out orders to one another, surgical tools were being passed around, and countless bloody bits of gauze littered the floor.

Hassan lay on the operating table with his chest cavity split wide open. Dr. Kemble worked hard removing the bullet from his chest. It was lodged a centimeter away from his heart, so it was a delicate procedure. Once the bullet was removed, the surgeon had to remove the damaged part of Hassan's lung for him to breathe.

Dion sat in the waiting room praying that Hassan would pull through. She didn't know how she was going to make it without him in her life.

"Mrs. Johnson?" An older white male walked up to her.

Dion looked at him with stress-filled eyes and was almost sure where this conversation was about to go.

"I'm Detective Murphy. We spoke briefly last night at your home before you got the call about your husband. I was—"

"I hate to be rude, but can't you see that I'm dealing with something?" she snapped, cutting the detective off. "You already have my statement, and no, I don't have anything more to tell you! So please, just leave me alone!"

The detective could see the hurt pouring out of her eyes and didn't want to agitate her more than what he'd done thus far. Experience had taught him that witnesses and victims were more reluctant to cooperate when they were upset. "Well, I'll leave you my card. If you can think of anything else, just give me a call." He pointed out his cell number on the card, then walked off.

Just as he was leaving, Nasir came running through the lobby of the hospital. "Mom!" Nasir called out when he saw Dion.

She stood up, and he wrapped his arms around her. She needed his shoulder to cry on, and Nasir only wished that there were something he could do to take his mother's pain away. Trying his best to console her, he said, "He's gonna be all right. It's Hassan."

"Mrs. Johnson?" someone called out.

At first Dion thought it was the detective again and was just about to give him a piece of her mind. But when she looked up, she saw Dr. Kemble walking toward her. Instinctively, she braced herself for the worst.

"Your husband is alive, but he's in critical condition. He suffered a significant amount of damage to his chest, and the bullet that grazed his head caused his brain to swell," the doctor explained.

Just listening to the injuries alone caused Dion to break down. Nasir had to hold her.

The doctor didn't want to leave her with the notion there was no hope for Hassan. In fact, he was a little optimistic. "Look, Mrs. Johnson. I'm going to be honest with you. He has a good chance of pulling through, but the next few hours are going to be critical for him. If he can hold on for another day or two, the chances of recovery will be a lot higher," he explained. "Now he's in the intensive care unit, but I'll permit immediate family members to visit him."

Dion thanked him before he walked off, and she was escorted to the ICU.

Detectives White and Smith stood in front of the task force they had assembled. The news of Hassan being shot really put a halt to their investigation. The unfortunate part about it was that when one boss fell, another rose.

"What about Ricky?" Detective Mills suggested, pulling his picture out of the pile. Ricky managed the Logan section of the city for Hassan. He was good with money and wasn't the flashy type, which made for a good leader.

"I'm almost sure that Shy is next in line," Detective Smith cut in. Shy was Hassan's top shooter, and damn near all of North Philly knew of him and were scared to death of his brutal ways.

"Plus, he was with Hassan when he got shot, which he'll use to his advantage in some kind of way," Smith continued.

He had a good point. There were times when Shy held court on the streets. He executed a man in broad daylight on Broad Street, and not one person was brave enough to tell on him.

"Nah. Ricky and Shy go hard without a doubt, but trust me when I tell you that this will be the next person who steps up and takes the reins," Detective White said. He pulled Sarita's picture from the pile and pinned it up on the bulletin board.

"What makes you think it's gonna be her?" Smith asked, looking up at the photo.

"When Hassan was on house arrest, he didn't have Ricky or Shy handling his business on the streets. Hell, he didn't even have his own brother, Chuck, out there. But guess who was?" White asked with a smile on his face.

Simultaneously, Mills and Smith said, "Sarita!"

"She was the one who ran around the city making sure that the product got out on the streets. And two of my informants said that she, of everybody who works for Hassan, has the best chance of taking his place," Detective White explained.

After hearing that, nobody in the room could argue with him. Nobody could come up with anyone else who had a better chance to lead. And just like that, Sarita was at the top of the investigation—a place she wasn't ready to be.

"How about we go and check up on Hassan? That is if he's still alive. Maybe he'll want to talk now," Detective White said, then grabbed his jacket and headed for the door.

Chapter 21

It'd been two weeks since the night of the shooting, and Sarita hadn't heard from Dion or from Nasir. However, she did get the word that Hassan had survived the shooting. She was more curious as to why she wasn't in jail yet, or even dead for that matter. As far as she was concerned, she wasn't about to let that stop the progress she'd been making in the streets with getting the dope back from Camille. That was a job in and of itself.

"Wow, Sarita! This place is nice!" Shay said, doing a 360-degree turn in the condo. This was the first time Sarita had anyone in her condo, and who better than her best friend? "So where's my room?" Shay asked while playfully dancing her way over to Sarita, who was at the minibar.

Sarita put down the bottle of scotch, grabbed Shay's hand, and led her down the hallway. "Now I had this room painted white so you'll be able to decorate it the way you like." Sarita opened the bedroom door. It was huge and had a picture window with a beautiful view of the neighborhood. It also had its own bathroom and walk-in closet. She had Shay's name carved into the wooden vanity mirror that was leaning in the corner of the room.

Shay was only joking about having her own room, but it appeared that Sarita already had in mind that she was going to live with her. "You really want me to live here wit' you?" Shay asked.

"Hell no!" Sarita laughed. "You got ya own house, but whenever you wanna stay here, this is your room," she said. She pulled out a key and a parking pass from her pocket.

Shay turned and gave Sarita a huge hug and a bunch of kisses on her cheek.

A knock at the door caught their attention. Sarita wasn't expecting anybody, but at the same time, she didn't think anything of it. When she opened the door, there was a delivery woman from FedEx.

"I have a delivery for Sarita Powell," the woman said. It had Dion's law firm as the return address. Sarita opened the package. Inside was a CD case with a note attached:

> *He wasn't who you thought he was. And whenever you get a chance, your father would like to see you.*

Now Sarita's curiosity was piqued. Not only was Hassan still alive, but he wanted to see her. Then there was the DVD. "Give me a minute," she told Shay. She took the DVD to her room.

She inserted the DVD and pressed the play button. When the footage came on, she stepped back and took a seat on the bed. It was a homemade movie, the same one that Dion had watched. Sarita could identify everyone in the film, including her mother. It was Hassan, Chuck, Camille, and another woman. Sarita just sat there watching attentively the entire time.

After a while of not seeing too much of anything except for sexual activities, she was about to fast-forward the DVD. She wasn't too enthused about hearing how Hassan planned to have sex with Dion. But things really got interesting.

The camera was still rolling and caught Camille exiting the bathroom with nothing but a towel on. She seemed unaware that she was being recorded. She climbed onto the bed and pulled Hassan's dick through his boxers. Sarita turned her head, not wanting to see her mother suck her father's dick. Then Hassan began fucking Camille, and that was when Sarita had enough. She hopped up from the bed to eject the DVD, but before she could press the button, she jumped at the sound of a gunshot coming from the TV. She looked back at the footage and saw Chuck stumbling into the room with a gun in his hand. He was yelling, "We gotta get da fuck outta here! Let's go!"

The footage showed Hassan jumping out of the bed and putting his clothes on. Camille did the same thing, not knowing what was going on. She ran out of the room behind Hassan, and you could clearly hear Hassan asking Chuck what had happened. Then there was a loud scream, and Sarita knew that it had come from Camille. Hassan ran back into the room and grabbed the camera, and that was when the footage ended.

Sarita sat there on her bed with her mouth wide open. What she had eaten for lunch spewed out of her mouth. She threw up all over the floor. Her heart sank into her now empty stomach, and as it registered in her brain, the realization of what she did to her father hit her like a ton of bricks. Not only did she try to kill an innocent man, but that innocent man was her biological father.

All these years she was fed lies after lies about him, ultimately leading up to her trying to kill him. Camille had everybody fooled.

Everything that had taken place that night was consensual, and it seemed like Camille was enjoying herself very much up to the point when Chuck burst into the room. The more she thought about it, the more she was hurt, and the more she was hurt, the more angered she became.

Dion and Nasir stood outside of the hospital. They were unconcerned about the rain. It had been a little more than a week since Hassan was shot, and for Dion, things weren't getting any easier. She was fortunate enough to be there when Hassan did crack open his eyes for the first time. She even got to say a few words to him, and vice versa. Even though the doctor said that Hassan wasn't in critical condition anymore, there was still the possibility that he could slip back into a coma, and that was what Dion feared the most, especially not knowing how Hassan ended up getting shot in the first place. Until this day, the only people who knew what happened to him in the back of the club were he and Sarita, which was frustrating.

"You good, Mom?" Nasir asked, seeing his mom looking dazed. "He's gonna be all right. He's out of the woods. Doc said he can only get better from here on out."

Dion stood there listening while her tears mixed with the rain that had beaded up on her face. She knew how Nasir felt about Hassan before the rape allegations, and that was the main reason she'd told him everything that had transpired thus far.

The McLaren engine could be heard pulling up to the hospital, and when Nasir looked up, Sarita's car was coming to a stop. She stepped out of the car and threw her hood over her head and walked over to where they were standing. Nasir let out a frustrated sigh and walked away. He still felt some type of way about her not telling his mother what happened the night Hassan was shot, and since she wasn't talking, Nasir didn't have anything to say to her.

Walking over and standing next to Dion, Sarita said, "I see he's still mad at me."

"Can you blame him? It's been over a week, and we still don't know what happened to my husband," Dion replied, looking up at the hospital.

Sarita didn't want to lie to Dion, and telling her the truth wasn't an option. If it was up to her, shooting Hassan was going to her grave with her unless Hassan had told Dion, which he hadn't, for reasons unknown to Sarita.

"I got ya package today, but I'm curious why you sent the video to me. What was your purpose behind it?"

Dion remained silent for a moment, obviously thinking about Hassan. "I sent that to you because I thought you should know the truth," she said. "Also, since I'm putting you on a need-to-know basis, I thought I'd let you know that I'ma kill ya mother. And since you saw the video, I'm quite sure you know why."

Sarita was surprised that Dion was so blunt about her intentions. She wanted to kill her mother too, but hearing that coming from Dion put her on the defense. Camille had fucked up royally, but at the end of the day, she was still Sarita's mother. "So what do you expect me to do while you're killing my mother?" she asked.

For the first time since she'd been there, Dion turned to face Sarita. "I really don't care what you do. But I'm only going to warn you once, Sarita. Don't get involved, because I swear that if you do, I'ma kill you too," she said with conviction in her eyes.

This definitely wasn't the way Sarita thought the conversation was going to go when she pulled up. Nevertheless, it happened, and there was nothing more to say. This was the beginning of something that would turn ugly. Sarita turned to walk away, almost forgetting why she was there.

Dion had to remind her. "Are you going up to see Hassan?"

Sarita thought about it, looked at the walls of the hospital, and shook her head. "Nah, I'll see him another day. I got some business to attend to."

Chapter 22

Camille and Isis stood in front of SK's grave. Camille had to admit she really missed SK, despite that she was the one who actually took his life. Only being honest with herself, she was falling in love with him, but the love she had for Sarita was much stronger.

"I'm sorry for your loss," Isis said, looking down at his plot.

Camille stood there, and for a moment she almost felt like shedding a tear.

The McLaren could be heard coming through the cemetery, and when Sarita's car came to a stop about twenty-five yards away, Camille let out a frustrated sigh, not really wanting to deal with Sarita. It was also a little disrespectful that Sarita would show up there.

"Hey, Sarita," Isis greeted her when Sarita walked over.

Camille didn't say anything but rather wondered if the gun she had in her Gucci bag had a bullet in the chamber.

"Hey, Isis," Sarita returned. "Ay, let me holla at Camille for a second."

Isis didn't have a problem with it and gave Sarita a hug before walking over to Camille's car.

"So wassup? I hear ya father's gonna pull through," Camille began.

Sarita wasn't about to play any games with her. She wanted to get straight to business. "I always knew you were a liar. And it's crazy, because my gut was telling me all these years that there were two sides to ya story."

"About what?" Camille snapped back.

"About my father. He never raped you. As a matter of fact, you gave it up."

"He did rape me!" Camille countered.

Sarita became furious. She pulled the chrome snub-nosed .38 from her pocket and held it down by her side. "I saw the fuckin' tape!" she said through clenched teeth.

This violent proposal changed everything, and in an instant, Camille no longer looked at Sarita as her daughter but rather a threat she might have to neutralize. "You pulled a gun on me?"

"You must have lost ya fuckin' mind! I want my dope back, and I want you to leave the city!" Sarita said with a serious look on her face.

Camille laughed at the demand for her to leave Philly. That comment jeopardized Sarita getting the dope back as well. "And what if I say no?"

Sarita looked at the large amount of space next to SK's grave and said, "I'ma bury you right here next to your boyfriend." She raised the gun and pointed it at Camille's face.

Camille's heart began to race out of fear, but she wasn't going to let Sarita see it. "See, if you kill me, you know you're gonna have to kill her too." She nodded toward her car.

When Sarita looked, Isis's face was glued to the window with nothing but fear in her eyes. She didn't have a problem killing Camille if she didn't want to comply, but never did she imagine she would have to kill Isis too.

Camille banked on that as well. "Look, I'ma return most of ya dope to where I got it from, but I'm not leaving Philly. If you kill me, then that's the way it's gonna be. I'll call you when it's done." She turned and walked away from Sarita, no longer worried about being shot.

Sarita tucked the gun back into her pocket and waited for Camille to get into her car. A clear statement was made by both of them. Neither one was going to back down.

Camille pulled up to the Honeycomb Hideout, a place where SK and his boys normally met up within the projects. There had to be at least twenty men standing outside, and from the look of the way they were standing, she knew that each and every one of them was carrying a gun. A couple of SK's hood rats were also there, but none of that stopped Camille from getting out of the car and walking through the crowd like she wasn't the one who shot their leader.

"Are you going to step aside, or are we gonna have a problem?" Camille asked Big Chris, who was standing in front of the apartment door like he was a bouncer. His reason—along with everyone else's reason—for standing around was to protect the person inside.

Before Camille could continue, the front door opened, and coming from behind Big Chris was Mega, SK's little brother. "Stand down. Y'all know who this is?" he asked rhetorically.

Most of them knew who Camille was and only needed to be reminded that she was SK's girl. Big Chris stepped to the side and allowed Camille to enter the apartment with Mega.

"Niggas are on edge right now," Mega began to explain. "Since my brother got murdered, the whole projects are expecting me to take his place, but I don't have a clue about what's going on out here in these streets." He had been out of the projects for a couple of years now, so his knowledge about SK's operation was limited. Still, the hood thought he was to be their savior.

Camille saw an opportunity to capitalize on the situation and decided to try her hand. "I think I might be able to help you out," she said, taking a seat next to him on the couch. "I just need you to do one thing before I can help you."

"Yeah? What is it?"

There were several people standing outside who needed to support Camille before she could do anything. Big Chris was one of them, along with Shooter, Dice, and Rec. Those four men had a lot of influence over the projects, and without their backing, her plans would be dead in the water. The only thing she had going for her was Mega, probably the only person who could tell them to take orders from her. Their loyalty to SK reached deep into his bloodline and landed right on Mega's lap. His word was binding.

Confused as to what actions she should take right now, Sarita sat in her car looking out her window at people walking in and out of the hospital. All sorts of thoughts ran through her mind.

"You want me to go check it out first?" Shay asked, seeing that Sarita really didn't want to go inside.

"No, it's all right," she replied. She turned her car off and opened the door. Shay followed her as they made their way into the hospital.

Hassan was still in the intensive care unit fighting for his life. When Sarita finally made it to his room, Dion and Nasir were at his bedside as expected, and Sarita could feel a not-too-warm welcome when she entered the room. Shay waited outside but was attentive to what was going on inside.

"How is he?" Sarita asked, standing at the foot of the bed and looking down at her father. Tears instantly began to fill her eyes at the thought of what she'd done to him. He had a tube shoved down his throat, wires hooked up to him, and a thick white bandage wrapped around his head where the bullet grazed him.

"The doctor said that it's totally up to him whether he pulls through. They've done all they can do," Nasir explained.

The entire time he explained the prognosis, Dion sat there with an irritated look on her face. She wasn't in a position to prove it, but deep down inside she knew Sarita was the reason Hassan was on his deathbed. With Sarita standing there before her, Dion wasn't going to miss out on the opportunity to ask a few questions. "Did you see him that night? Did Hassan ever come and get you?" she asked.

The question took Sarita by surprise. She didn't know Dion knew about the rescue operation Camille had put together. She shook her head no, not sure of what else Dion knew.

"So how did you get free?" Dion asked.

Nasir looked from his mother to Sarita with a confused look on his face. "Mom, what are you talking about?"

Sarita couldn't come up with a lie fast enough. It made Dion even more upset.

"You still didn't tell him?" Dion asked, cutting her eyes over at Nasir.

Sarita had a pleading look in her eyes. She didn't want Dion to expose her right now.

But Dion couldn't care less. "She's his daughter," she said with a single tear dropping from her eye.

Nasir had a confused look on his face and looked over at Sarita.

"Yeah. Ya mother told me all about you," Dion continued.

The whole room became quiet as Dion's words marinated.

Nasir rose to his feet with an even more confused look on his face. "So you mean to tell me that Hassan is ya father?" he asked. He looked for some type of answer from her, but Sarita couldn't even look him in the eyes.

"Yes, he's my father, but I just—"

Nasir put his hand up so Sarita would stop talking. He couldn't stand to hear another word come out of her mouth, let alone be in the same room as her. He stormed out, bumping Sarita with his shoulder as he walked past.

He was heated and confused about this, and Sarita knew him well enough to know that time and space were what he needed right now instead of her chasing him.

Dion still wanted answers, but Sarita wasn't in the mood to talk. She gave it a couple of minutes, then she too left Hassan's room, but not before giving Hassan a kiss on the forehead.

Isis was scared to death sitting in the car by herself. She let out a sigh of relief when Camille exited the apartment. "Damn, Mom! Are you okay?" she asked when Camille got into the car.

Camille had a look of sorrow on her face, but on the inside she felt the opposite. Mega had Shooter, Dice, Big Chris, and Rec now answering to her since she knew SK's whole operation. She even convinced Mega that she had a connect who would supply her with both coke and heroin, and it seemed like in an instant she was the help he needed.

"Isis, when are ya father's visiting days?" she asked, knowing that if anybody could plug her into a connect, he could.

"On Fridays, Saturdays, and Sundays. Why are you asking?"

Camille didn't want to let Isis know what was going on this early in the game, but at the same time she was going to need her to deliver messages to Chip, Isis's father, while he was in prison. An old felony conviction prevented Camille from being able to get on his visiting list, which left it all up to Isis. "I think it's time you pay ya dad a visit," she said as she pulled out of the projects.

Detective White walked into Hassan's hospital room, and Dion immediately went into defense mode. "I already gave my statement to the detective down at the station," she snapped. She thought he was there to ask about the murder that took place at their house, but that wasn't the case. Because he was investigating Hassan, his primary goal was to find out what happened to him.

"Look, I'm going to be straight with you, Dion." White took a seat by Hassan's bed. "That man who broke into your house? Well, he was someone of importance. Not only did he run half the city, he himself was a stone-cold killer. I don't think this is going to stop here."

"So what are you saying? Me and my family aren't safe here?" Dion asked. She wanted to see where the detective was going.

White held his hand up and confirmed what Dion was thinking.

Sarita walked into the room and heard the end of the conversation. "Well, if he's not safe, then nobody in this city is safe," she told the detective.

She turned to the door and nodded for her people to enter the room. Two men stood outside the room while another came in and posted up against the wall. Everybody was legally packing and was ready to go to war in order to keep Hassan safe. She looked over at Dion and said, "These men are going to stay with you until my father is strong enough to be transferred to another hospital. The last thing you gotta worry about is anybody coming up in here and doing something to him."

Both Dion and White were shocked at how hard Sarita came through.

"What did you just say? That's your father?" White asked and took out his pad and pen to write all of this down.

Sarita didn't bother answering him and looked at Dion to make sure she was okay with the security.

Dion was still angry and upset about Sarita's involvement, but at the same time she could see some genuine concern in her eyes, and she felt the security she provided for Hassan was necessary and right on time. She nodded, giving Sarita the okay to proceed.

Detective White sat there with a dumb look on his face and was dismissed by Dion before he could ask another question. In retaliation, he wanted to pat down everyone who was in the room, but he ultimately decided against it since it would have been an illegal search.

"Dion, I know you've got a lot of questions, and I give you my word that I'll answer all of them in due time. Right now, I have to go and make sure that the threat to my father is neutralized. The detective was right. SK's got some ruthless niggas on his team, and I'm not about to take any chances," Sarita explained.

Camille dropped Isis off at home so that she could get a good night's sleep before her trip to see her father in the morning.

Before Camille could drive off, she got a text message on her phone from Mega. She looked at the screen and couldn't believe her eyes: He lives to see another day!

To be certain that he was talking about Hassan, she texted back: Are you sure?

Mega hit her right back: As sure as water is wet.

Camille tossed the phone into the center console and leaned her head against the steering wheel. A million thoughts ran through her mind, but one seemed to stick out: the one where she'd hoped Hassan had died. But because that wasn't the case, she knew she had more than one or two problems on her hand.

Aside from Mega and his crew with their thirst for revenge, Camille feared Sarita more, because she didn't know what she was going to do once she found out the truth from Hassan—that was if she didn't already know. Camille went from being shocked to confused, and to being downright paranoid, and she had every reason to be, because Sarita was operating on a whole different level.

Chapter 23

Camille could feel the tension in the air the moment she walked through the door. Mega and his crew were standing around in the living room with nothing but malice in their eyes. She almost thought the stares were for her. "What's the problem now?" she asked and set her bag on the coffee table.

"Yeah, we got a little problem," Mega answered. "Everything's getting shut down until we take care of this situation."

Camille thought about the dope. "We don't have time to be dealing wit' the bullshit!" she shot back. "I got like thirty kilos of heroin to move—"

"We're not movin' no product until da nigga Hassan and his bitch get taken care of," Shooter cut in. "I wouldn't care if you had a hundred kilos of that shit!"

"And how do you suppose we're going to make that happen? He's in a coma, in the hospital, in the ICU, with police guarding his door. I'm more than sure his wife's got some type of security following her around everywhere she goes when she's not at the hospital. Plus, they have . . ." Camille paused before she mentioned Sarita's name, and it was like a lightbulb went off in her head.

Mega walked over to her with a curious look on his face. "What are you thinking about?" he asked.

Camille didn't want this, but it looked like the only way her life was going to move forward was if one thing happened. It was something she'd regret if it came to that, something that was sure to shed a lot of blood, and something that could possibly end her life in the process. "I think we gotta go to war with Hassan's people," she finally said.

Sarita sat on one side of Hassan's bed while Dion sat on the other. Most of Dion's questions had been answered concerning what was going on, but Sarita simply refused to tell her that she was the person who shot Hassan and had him lying there fighting for his life. Dion wasn't ready to hear something like that.

"You should go home and get some rest. Nothing's gonna happen to him," Sarita assured her.

"Nah, I can't go back to that house. The people came and cleaned up the blood, but it's still too soon."

"Well, you can stay at my place. I'll have Shay take you there. You can eat, shower, and grab a couple hours' sleep."

The offer was enticing. Dion was beginning to smell herself, not having taken a shower for the past couple of days. Sponge baths in Hassan's bathroom weren't really getting the job done. "Someone needs to be here with him at all times," she said.

"I'll be here. I'm not gonna leave his side."

On that, Dion took Sarita up on her offer and left.

To be there with Hassan was the least Sarita felt she could do. And for personal reasons, she was hoping she could be there when and if he woke up.

***

"Bro, I'm not trying to tell you how to run ya shit—"

"Well, don't!" Mega said, cutting Shooter off. Ever since the news came back that Hassan was still alive, dudes in the projects were out for blood. They were ready to pounce but couldn't move unless Mega gave the word. At the moment, he wasn't ready to make that call. Unlike SK, he was a thinker and didn't just move impulsively. Plus, when it came to taking someone's life, he was the type to make sure he got his man and not some innocent bystander. "I just need some time to think some shit through," he explained. "I'm not gonna have y'all running around hurting innocent people."

"Yo, Mega, I know you haven't been out here in a while, but honestly speaking, we don't give a fuck about who we hurt just as long as we kill Hassan and the bitch who killed your brother. There's no way possible SK should be in the ground and dem niggas are still breathing. It makes us look weak."

Mega could hear the hurt and concern in Shooter's voice, and though he wasn't as heartless as some of the people in the room, he did believe in revenge. It was a natural feeling, one that he couldn't control. "Listen, grab the homies and bring 'em back here. Let's come up with a way to get dis shit done quickly and quietly and with a minimum to no casualties on our side," he explained.

"That's wassup, bro!" Shooter said, rising to his feet. He gave Mega some dap and got right on the job of going to find Big Chris, Dice, and Rec so they could put in this work.

Sarita's phone started vibrating on her lap, waking her up from the hour-long nap she had taken in the chair next to Hassan's bed. She looked up to see that his condition was the same. The phone continued vibrating, and when she looked down at the screen, Torres's number flashed. She got up and walked away from Hassan's bedside to answer it.

"*Hola, papi!*" she greeted him in a low tone.

"*Hola, mami!* I need to see you. I was hoping you could stop by tonight."

Sarita let out a sigh. She knew he wanted to talk business, and with the loss she'd just taken with Camille, she wasn't in a position to negotiate anything. Nevertheless, when the boss wanted to speak to you, you just couldn't say no. "I'll see you in a couple of hours, *papi,*" she said and ended the call.

She immediately called Shay to see where she and Dion were. They'd been gone for almost five hours now.

"We just left the house," Shay said after answering her phone. "We should be there in a minute. Oh, and Dion wants to know if Hassan woke up yet. You're on speaker." She held up the phone so Dion could hear.

"No, he hasn't woken up yet. The doctor came in and checked on him. He said they might be removing some fluid from his brain tomorrow," Sarita explained. "Other than that, it's quiet. I'll see y'all when you get back. I just wanted to check up on y'all."

Sarita walked back over to Hassan's bedside. Every time she looked at him, her eyes began to fill with tears of guilt. She reached down and gently placed her hand inside of his, hoping that he would squeeze it or do anything to show that he was still in there. Although he never responded, she remained confident he was going to make it through.

Chapter 24

Tina was cutting the last two kilos of heroin on the kitchen table when she heard a loud knock at the door. She snapped her fingers at one of the workers, telling him to grab the Mack-90 from under the couch.

"Who is it?" she asked while looking through the peephole with a .50-caliber Desert Eagle clutched in her hand.

"I'm dropping something off for ya boss," a female answered from the other side.

Tina looked at her worker, then cautiously cracked open the door. Camille was standing there with a duffle bag over her shoulder and another duffle bag on the porch. Her car was double-parked in the middle of the street.

"Are you gonna grab these bags, or am I supposed to stand out here with a hundred kilos of heroin?" she asked in a sarcastic manner.

Tina looked at her, then looked at the bags. "We're not expecting any deliveries today," she told her with a suspicious look on her face.

"Just call Sarita. She's expecting this. And if I walk away with the product, I promise you I won't be returning," Camille warned.

Tina already had her phone out behind the door and was speed-dialing Sarita. "Hold on," she told Camille, and then closed the door. "Yo, Sarita, was you expecting a package today?" she asked when Sarita answered her phone.

Sarita made Tina describe the carrier, and once she determined that it was Camille bringing the dope back, she gave her the green light to accept the package.

Tina opened the door so Camille could come inside. When she did, she tossed both of the bags in the center of the living room floor, turned around, and walked back out.

"Everything better be here, too," Tina mumbled to herself after closing the door behind Camille.

The worker walked back to the kitchen while Tina inspected the contents of the bag. "Finish the rest of that," she called out to the worker, then began to unzip one of the duffle bags.

An unusual sound came from the bag as she unzipped it. It was sort of like a key being turned in a lock. When she opened the bag, the last thing she saw was a grenade sitting on top of the heroin.

Boooom!

The explosion rocked the entire house and the houses next door in both directions. The force of the blast nearly split Tina in half, knocking her across the room. Black smoke quickly filled the house, and the couch went up in flames almost instantly.

Sarita didn't understand why Torres picked an airport as the place for them to meet up. He never made mention that they were flying anywhere. Inside the hangar were two Range Rovers and a G4 jet.

"*Hola, mami!*" Torres greeted her as he emerged from the jet. He was wearing a white Tom Ford suit and a huge smile on his face.

"*Hola, Torres!*" Sarita greeted him in return. "What's going on? You planning on leaving the country?" she asked, pointing to the plane.

"Come on and walk with me." He grabbed her hand and walked her to the back of the hangar where they could speak in private. "First, I want to tell you that I'm impressed with how you took over Hassan's organization almost singlehandedly. I have to admit I didn't think you could pull it off."

"Yeah, well, there's still work to be done. I got a few things to take care of before I can take a victory lap." Sarita was referring to Camille and any other threats that were lurking out there.

"I'm sure you'll be successful. That's why I'm going to offer you the opportunity of a lifetime."

"A lifetime?" Sarita repeated with a raised eyebrow.

"You know my business stretches far beyond the States. I want you to be my face in Africa," he explained.

"Africa?" Sarita asked in shock. "Are you serious? That's the other side of the world!"

"Yes. The heroin is potent and cheap over there. You only have to fly out to Mali once a month, check out the product, shake a few hands, and then fly back to the States."

Sarita was still trying to process the whole Africa thing.

"I promise you, Sarita, if you work for me, I'll make you the richest eighteen-year-old in America."

The offer sounded nice, but Sarita still couldn't get over the Africa thing. "I'll need some time to think about it, Torres," she said.

Torres smiled and looked down at his watch. This wasn't the type of offer that would come back around. His vision for her was major, and she needed to act on it now or never. "I'll give you a few minutes to think about it. The offer stands until the engine starts." He walked onto the plane.

Sarita felt that she was about to miss out on a great opportunity. "And when am I supposed to start?" she called out to Torres.

"You start now!"

The bombing at Tina's house made the news, and they were running live coverage as the bomb squad was on the scene clearing the house of any other possible bombs. Shay got the phone call from a worker telling her what went down, and within minutes she was on the scene, along with over a hundred civilians. "Come on, Sarita! Answer your phone!" she said, but the calls kept going straight to voicemail every time she tried.

"There might be terrorists up in there!" one onlooker yelled out of ignorance. Shay wanted to tell the girl to shut up but didn't because somebody had beat her to it.

Shay's phone rang. She quickly looked at the ID hoping it was Sarita. It was Rando. "Yeah, wassup?" she answered.

"Yo, where is Sarita?" he yelled through the phone. "Muthafuckas just came through here shootin' shit up! Quil got hit!"

Shay could hear people yelling in the background through Rando's phone. She was also shouting, telling him the shooters might be coming back around. "I'm on my way," she told Rando, then stayed on the line as she began to push through the crowd of people. By the time she got to her car, the phone went dead. "What da fuck is going on?" Shay asked herself.

She tried to call Sarita again. "Come on, Sarita!" The call went straight to voicemail again, only frustrating her more. She couldn't believe what was going down, and Sarita was nowhere to be found. As second-in-command, Shay was going to have to step up and restore some order in the streets—a task she wasn't sure she was capable of.

Detective White let out a whistle when he saw Tina's body lying on the coroner's table. The bomb blew half of her left torso off and melted the skin on most of her body. It was gruesome to look at, but he and Detective Smith listened as the medical examiner explained in detail why and how the blast caused as much damage as it did.

Smith pointed out some odd-looking fluid on the melted skin. "It's heroin," the medical examiner told him, taking a pair of tweezers and pulling a piece of it off to show them.

That was one thing Detective White couldn't understand about the case. *Why would anyone blow up this much heroin?* he kept asking himself. The street value of what was in the two bags was hundreds of thousands of dollars. "Do we still have eyes on Sarita?" he asked Smith.

"No. They lost her at the airport. As far as they know, she could be somewhere in the city. I know one thing though—she's gonna be pissed off when she finds out about her heroin."

"Yeah, and we gotta find a way to link her to all of this. If she's the one calling the shots right now, it's definitely going to show."

***

Shay got out of her car on Thirty-ninth Street with a black Glock 9 mm in her hand. After all that transpired earlier today, she definitely wasn't taking any chances rolling around without a gun.

"Did you see her yet?" Rell asked when she walked up.

"Nah, not yet. I think her battery might be dead or something. But wassup wit' y'all? Is everything good over here?" She kept a watchful eye out for the crackheads walking up and down the street.

"It's been quiet over here, but you already know we stay ready." Rell nodded across the street at one of his workers standing against the wall under a tree. It was so dark over there Shay could barely see him. "How about you? You good? You know you shouldn't be riding around by yourself."

Shay smiled, then flashed the gun she had in her hand. "I'm never by myself."

Rell smiled with respect.

She walked back to her car and stopped at the driver-side door. The hairs on the back of her neck stood up. She looked up and down the street only to see a crackhead coming down the street and a couple of workers by the Chinese store on the corner. Something wasn't right. The grip she had on her gun became tighter, and when a car turned onto the street, it got her undivided attention.

The dark-colored vehicle drove by, and Shay watched attentively until she realized it wasn't a threat. She turned around to say something to Rell, and the person she thought was a crackhead had a gun pointed at his head. It was Shooter. Rell wasn't paying attention, and for Shay it was like time had slowed up for a minute.

Rell saw the expression on Shay's face, but by the time he turned around to see what was going on, Shooter had pulled the trigger. Pop!

Shooter wasted no time turning his gun on Shay, and he fired several shots in her direction. The worker who was across the street took off running without firing a single shot. Shay took cover behind the car, but Shooter was relentless, firing several more rounds into her vehicle as he walked up to it.

Shay didn't want to go out like this. She jumped up from behind her car and let bullets fly.

Pop! Pop! Pop! Pop!

Shooter wasn't expecting her to start firing. He jumped behind a car.

Shay took the opportunity to move down the street with her gun aimed in Shooter's direction. When she turned to run, she ran straight into a thirty-two-shot TEC aimed at her face.

Click!

Camille's gun had misfired.

Shay froze for a second, giving Camille time to cock a bullet into the chamber. When she did that, the TEC jammed. Shay didn't even think to shoot her, but instead took off running.

Shooter was going to chase her down, but a couple of the corner boys came running down the street with guns in their hands.

Camille smacked the side of the gun, trying to get it to unjam. Realizing they were outnumbered, Camille and Shooter took off running in the opposite direction, crouching behind cars as bullets whizzed by their heads.

Chapter 25

Sarita held on to the rails as the Jeep Wrangler maneuvered through the rugged terrain of the Mali jungle. Torres was being escorted in another Jeep right behind her. He had a small army of African jungle men as their personal security. Groups like Boko Haram would sometimes use the jungle to transport weapons and such, and if they ever came across people like Torres or Sarita, they would surely kidnap them and hold them for a high ransom.

"Almost there!" the driver yelled over the rumble of the caravan.

This was all too surreal for her, and reality was only about to hit her harder.

After an hour-long drive, the Jeep finally came to a stop. For the first time since the beginning of the ride, she could see the sun. It had been hidden behind all the trees, but now it was clear as day, shining over several acres of farmland. "Damn!" she exclaimed, looking out at the huge poppy fields that were guarded by armed men. There had to be well over a hundred men and women tending to the plants.

"This is where the real magic happens." Torres walked up behind her. He stood next to her, taking in the sight.

It wasn't long before a group of African men—several of whom were armed—approached, and Sarita could tell who was in charge right off the bat.

"Hello, my friend!" a man greeted Torres with a smile on his face.

"Kehmba! So nice to see you!" Torres returned. They embraced as two men with years of friendship between them.

Kehmba looked at Sarita with his arms crossed. "If you made it this far, he really must have a lot of faith in you. If I were you, I would make the best out of this exclusive opportunity." He turned back to Torres and looked him right in his eyes. "My friend, are you sure about this?" he asked with a serious look on his face.

Torres gave him a simple nod of his head. Had he done anything other than that, Sarita's body would have become one with the jungle.

"Okay, so let's get down to business." Kehmba waved for Sarita to follow him.

Torres stayed behind, allowing Sarita and Kehmba to feel each other out. This was the beginning stages of them building a business relationship, which was needed if Sarita ever had plans to make this trip again.

Kehmba was about to expose Sarita to something only a few people had ever experienced in their lifetime. She was about to be shown how heroin was grown, picked, processed, packed, and shipped to the United States by Africa's most powerful drug lord.

"Just shut everything down until we get a hold of Sarita," Shay told Rando, who couldn't stop pacing back and forth.

"Ain't no telling where she's at. For all we know, she could be dead too," Rando shot back.

Shay stood up and stopped Rando in his tracks. "Don't ever let me hear you say some dumb shit like that again!"

Rando saw that Shay wasn't messing around either.

Shay was angry at the comment, even though a part of her thought about the possibility as well. Sarita hadn't called, her phone was off, and she hadn't been home in days. She didn't know what else she could do. "Like I said, everything is shut down until Sarita gets back," she repeated.

Shay's phone rang on the coffee table. The number was unavailable, and normally Shay wouldn't answer it, but today was different. "Yeah, who's this?" she answered with an attitude.

"Don't be answering ya phone like you crazy!" Sarita said.

Shay almost passed out when she heard her voice. "Oh, my God, Sarita! Where have you been? I've been trying to . . ." She could barely talk without tearing up. That was how happy she was to hear Sarita's voice.

"I know. I'm sorry. My phone died right before I got on the plane. It's still dead as we—"

"Plane? Where da hell are you?" she asked.

"It's a long story, but all you need to know right now is that we'll never be hungry again," Sarita said as she watched the workers packaging heroin.

All that was cool, but Shay had other things on her mind. "You need to get home like right now, Sarita!"

"We don't leave until later on tonight. Why? What's going on?"

Shay didn't want to go into detail over the phone. "Look, you just need to come home," she said.

Because Shay repeated this statement over and over again, Sarita knew that something bad must have happened back home. "A'ight, a'ight, Shay! I hear you! I'll be there as soon as I can. Do you still remember the protocol?" she asked.

Shay was already on point, as she was in the process of shutting everything down. Rando was the only one being hardheaded, but after the phone call that he'd witnessed, he too was going to comply with the order. Nothing else was going to move until Sarita got back to the States, and when she finally did come home, she was going to have her work cut out for her.

Dion walked into Hassan's hospital room with food from McDonald's. She nearly dropped it when she saw Hassan crack open his eyes and look directly at her. She tossed her things onto the chair and ran to his side. "Hi, baby!" she said with a soft voice before leaning in and kissing his forehead. She fought to not jump into the bed with him. "Baby, you're gonna be all right," she assured him.

Hassan couldn't keep his eyes open for a long period of time. He kept fading in and out until he eventually went back under. Dion didn't mind just as long as she was the first person he saw when he opened his eyes. Nothing else really mattered. She walked back over to the chair, pulled it over to his bedside, and began to eat her food. She wasn't going anywhere. If Hassan opened his eyes again, she wanted to be there.

Confused as to where Sarita was, Detectives White and Smith drove back to the airport, where the surveillance team had lost her. They got permission from the TSA to view the security footage from that day. It took a while, but they finally spotted her car. She had driven up to a private hangar, and when White asked the TSA agent where the plane was going, he told them that it was scheduled to leave for Africa.

After prying deeper as to who the private jet belonged to, the TSA agent refused to provide any more information. He told them that they would need a warrant from a judge in order to receive that information. The agent's unwillingness to help made White suspicious. It was as if the agent was trying to hide something.

As the detectives left the airport, Smith was frustrated. He wanted to do something he never wanted to do before: ask for assistance from the Feds.

"Yo, bro, I'm not the type to tell you any lies. The chick Camille goes hard in the paint. I mean, shorty put in work, and she looked good doing it," Shooter said to Mega.

The only thing Mega was worried about right now was getting to Hassan and his wife. That was his main objective. "They didn't move him yet, and the bitch Sarita is MIA right now."

Camille's had somewhat of a brain in her head, and she figured out that the only way she was going to satisfy SK's boys' thirst for blood was to draw Hassan out so they could kill him. The only way she was going to do that was by making Sarita and Dion feel like he wasn't safe in that particular hospital. With what was going on, Sarita would think that an attack on him was inevitable.

"Look, I need y'all to stay on point with this. When he moves, kill him. Kill him and her," Mega explained. "After this, I'm done with this shit. There's money to be made out here, and y'all niggas are making it hard to eat."

Mega made sense and was serious, too. But he wasn't feeling the whole "go to war" idea. All he wanted to do was make money, and if he was going to replace SK and take over his side of the city, this was a glimpse of how he was going to be running things.

Chapter 26

By the time Sarita made it back to the States, twenty-four hours had passed. The first place she went was the hospital to check on Hassan. She noticed the extra police presence in front of his door the moment she got there. There were also several men from her own crew.

Shay jumped up from her chair the moment she saw her. She ran up to Sarita and gave her a hug.

"What happened to your neck?" Sarita asked when she saw a speck of blood coming through a small bandage.

"That's what I need to talk to you about," Shay said, grabbing Sarita's hand and pulling her away from everybody. "Ya crazy-ass mother started a war. She's out of control. She killed Tina, blew up the heroin, and shot up Fifty-fourth, Fifty-sixth, and Forty-sixth Streets."

"Wait! Wait!" Sarita said, shaking her head. "You're talking about Camille?"

Shay nodded her head. "She had Rell killed and almost killed me in the process." She tilted her head so Sarita could see the bandage better. She hadn't realized that she'd been grazed until she got to Sarita's condo. "I wasn't sure if Camille would try to come here and do anything to Hassan, so I bulked up the security. And I don't know where the police came from. I think the hospital staff got scared of us."

"Don't worry about it. I'll take care of it," Sarita assured her. She gave Shay a hug, then headed for Hassan's room.

As expected, Dion was right by his side. Nasir was also in the room, but he was asleep in one of the chairs.

"Are you okay?" Dion asked her.

"Yeah, I'm good," Sarita replied in a low tone so she wouldn't wake up Nasir. "How is he?"

"He opened his eyes yesterday but went back under. The doctor said that's a good sign, but please don't ask me why."

Sarita looked over at Nasir and asked, "What about him?"

One of the worst things throughout this whole ordeal was hurting Nasir. She really did love him, and she still did to this very day. But despite that, if Hassan lived, they could never be together again. She felt it just wouldn't be ethical, a stepbrother and stepsister sleeping with each other. That was the hardest pill Sarita had to swallow.

"Dion, I know what I'm about to say may sound crazy, but I think we need to get my father out of this hospital. It's not safe here for him. It's not safe here for any of us," Sarita said. Knowing the people Camille was involved with, she knew that eventually Camille would try her hand. Sarita knew that with certainty, and before she let her kill Hassan, she was going to do everything in her power to make sure that it didn't happen. "Somebody get the doctor in here. I need to speak with him."

It had just started to rain when Camille pulled up to the projects and beeped her horn. Shooter jogged from his apartment and got into her car. She had more than enough time to think about the direction she was ready to take the projects in. She needed people within the projects to have the same or at least similar passions.

"Shooter, I like you and I have nothing but the utmost respect for you. However, I think it's time we had a serious conversation about the future of the projects."

"Yeah, I'm listening," Shooter responded.

"This whole 'going to war' thing is okay, but we're not making any money. Before you know it, we'll all be broke, and what will we have to show for all we're doing right now?"

Shooter sat there listening. He was already starting to feel the effects of business slowing up due to the lack of product. So what she was saying hit home a little.

"Look, I got enough dope to put us all the way in the game. All we have to do is move it. I'm supposed to be meeting up with a new connect in a couple of days, but I don't have the money."

Shooter already knew where she was going with that type of talk, and though it sounded good, it had nothing to do with the main objective, which was killing Hassan and Dion.

Camille was on point with that too, knowing that he would have some reservations about that. "I know you want Hassan dead, and believe me I do to. That's why I guarantee I will take care of that personally. You have my word. Look at me, Shooter," she said, wanting him to see how serious she was. "You of all people should know what I'm capable of. Hassan will die in the worst way."

Shooter could see in her eyes that she was telling the truth. It wasn't a question of whether she could get the job done, but rather when. He sat there thinking about it for a moment. "A'ight, we maybe can start moving the product, but I'ma hold you on ya word. And in this family, ya word is all you got," he concluded, then exited the car.

Camille was satisfied, and now it was time for her to put in some real work.

Sarita waited until nightfall before going outside. It was easier to maneuver under the cover of darkness. She put the McLaren up and was now driving a car that didn't draw any attention to her. It was a dark blue 1996 Bonneville. It definitely didn't draw any attention, nor was anybody in the hood familiar with her driving it.

Before driving off, she called Dion to advise her of the plan to move Hassan to a safer location.

"Sarita, the doctors don't advise it, but they said that Hassan is capable of being discharged from the hospital. Are you sure this is a good idea?" Dion asked, worried about the possible consequences.

"Yeah, I'm sure. We have to get him somewhere safe. Someone will be calling you in the next hour. Just follow his directions."

"What are you getting ready to do?" Dion asked.

"I'm about to have a conversation with my mother," Sarita said, ended the call with Dion, and drove off.

As she got closer to Camille's house, she needed to focus on the task at hand. She pulled up and parked on Fifty-eighth Street and quickly reached into the back seat. She grabbed a gym bag that contained a bulletproof vest and her gun. She looked up and down the street before pulling the vest over her head and tucking the .45 ACP into her waistband in the back. The two-block walk to Camille's house only took a minute or two. She prayed that her keys still worked.

Once she got up to the door, she drew her weapon. Her heart began to race once she saw that her key still worked. She entered the house as quietly as possible.

It was dark downstairs except for the kitchen light. Sarita could hear R&B playing upstairs on the radio, so she knew Camille had to be home. She eased her way up the steps with her gun pointed in front of her like she was a cop. Memories of all the hardships that had taken place in this house with her, Isis, and Camille flashed through her mind. The yelling, beatings for no reason, and all the other drama she went through with Isis were just a few things she thought about.

Sarita approached Camille's door and could hear loud moans mixed in with the music. She eased the door open without disturbing the two people under the blanket. The back of a man's head was all she could see. She had it in her mind that she was going to kill both of them, but before she did, she wanted Camille to see the person who was pulling the trigger. She got to the foot of the bed, aimed her gun at them, then reached down and yanked the comforter off the bed. She was two seconds away from opening fire, but right before she did, Isis poked her head out from under the guy.

Torres and a few of his friends were enjoying the night at Club 321. He didn't go out much, but when he did, he made sure he did it big. He bought out the bar, took over the VIP sections, and brought his very own strippers to entertain him and his friends. He even paid the DJ to play reggaeton music most of the night.

"Yo, *papi!* Check it out!" one of his men said, pointing to Camille, who was approaching the VIP section they were in.

Camille had Big Chris and Shooter with her, but that didn't stop Torres's men from stopping them at the entrance. "I need to speak to Torres!" she shouted over the music. "It's important!"

Torres motioned for one of his men to go over and pat them down to make sure they didn't have any weapons on them. Only Camille was allowed to enter while Big Chris and Shooter stayed up front.

Torres made room for her on the couch. "You better have a good reason why you're ruining my night!"

"I do. My brother told me that you could help me."

"And who is your brother?" Torres asked and took a sip of the champagne he had in front of him.

"Wink."

Hearing that name got Torres's undivided attention. He turned to take a closer look at Camille to see if she resembled him. She did. He couldn't believe it. He actually began to remember Camille from when she was younger. "How is he?" he asked.

"He's good, considering he's doing a life sentence for you."

Around ten years ago, Wink took a major drug case for Torres when Torres started out. Not only did Wink take a case for him, he never mentioned Torres's name to the Feds when they interrogated him, not even when the Feds offered to let him walk right out the door if he helped bring Torres in. Things like loyalty and honor meant more to him than being a snitch.

"Tell me, Camille, what can I do for you?"

Camille smiled at the fact that Torres remembered her name. "I need a new connect. I can have a million dollars by next week."

"And what are you looking for?"

"I want cocaine."

Torres sat in silence, thinking. He had access to it all: cocaine, heroin, weed, and pills. Getting Camille what she needed wasn't an issue. "I may be able to help you out. Give my man your number on ya way out, and I'll be contacting you soon."

Camille nodded her head and said, "Thank you."

"No problem. Next time you talk to Wink, let him know I'll be waiting for him."

Camille smiled, then turned around and walked off. She was in the game, and all she had to do now was come up with some money.

Isis sat on the edge of Camille's bed listening to Sarita explain all the foolishness that was going on between her and Camille. The guy Isis had over left in a hurry after almost losing his life.

"Damn, cousin! I didn't know my mom did you like that!" Isis said.

Sarita thought about it, and although she didn't want to be the one who told her, the full truth about who Camille was had to be told. "Isis, I need to tell you something, and it's probably going to be the worst news you ever heard. But I love you, and I'm always going to be here for you."

"What's going on?" Isis asked with a confused look on her face.

"Camille isn't who you think she is."

"What are you talking about?"

Sarita paused for a moment to collect her thoughts. "Camille isn't your mother," Sarita began. "She's actually my mother."

Isis started to chuckle, thinking that Sarita was playing. But the stern look in her eyes made Isis become serious. "You're playing, right?"

Sarita shook her head no and fought back the tears that filled her eyes. She explained everything her grandmother said about the family's secrets and lies. It took Isis by surprise, and as she sat there listening, all she could do was cry. It hurt, but Sarita knew that she deserved the truth, something no one else in the family was willing to tell her.

"I know this is a lot for you to take in, and like I said before, I'm here for you if you need me. But I really have to go, Isis."

"Where are you going?"

"I'm going to put an end to all of this," Sarita told her before stuffing the gun back into her waistband.

"Sarita, I know you're mad at Camille right now, but don't you think a gun is going a little overboard? I mean, what do you plan on doing when you do catch up to her? Are you planning on killing your own mother?"

"I really don't know what I plan on doing," Sarita lied. Her true intentions were clear. As soon as the opportunity presented itself, she was going to put a bullet in Camille's head. She just didn't want to tell Isis that because she wouldn't understand.

As Sarita was walking out of the room, something caught her attention. It was a familiar smell she couldn't ignore. She had to investigate further, so she took a deeper whiff and turned her head in its direction.

Isis looked on, confused as to what was going on. The smell got stronger as Sarita walked toward the closet.

"Sarita?" Isis said, but was shushed by her cousin.

Opening the closet door, Sarita didn't notice anything out of the ordinary. But after moving several shoeboxes and digging through some old clothes, she saw that a piece of the carpet had been cut in the back of the closet. The scent got stronger, and she knew it had to be here.

Pulling the carpet up, she found a small latch, and when she pulled it, a trapdoor opened up. When she looked into the cubbyhole, there it was: a couple of black duffle bags. She opened one of the bags to see kilos of heroin. "Jackpot!" she exclaimed.

"You dumb bitch! Why didn't you stop her?" Camille screamed and grabbed a lamp off the nightstand and threw it at Isis.

Isis attempted to run out of the bedroom, but Camille grabbed her and threw her up against the wall. She'd never seen Camille this upset, especially with her.

"What are you good for?" Camille screamed and wrapped her hands around Isis's neck and began choking her. "You let that bitch come up in here and take my shit!"

Camille expected Isis to put up some sort of fight or even simply try to defend herself, but there was nothing. Isis stood there, and as Camille looked into her eyes, she saw something more horrifying than the fear she wanted to instill in her. Camille saw hurt, something she'd never seen in Isis before. It made her loosen her grip around her neck.

But Isis protested by grabbing Camille's wrists and encouraging her to keep choking her. "Do it! Do it! Kill me! I fuckin' hate you!" Isis yelled. Then she began crying, thinking about everything Sarita had told her. It wasn't until after Sarita left that she began thinking about the totality of the circumstances, and the reality of her being motherless.

"What's going on with you?" Camille asked, snatching her hands away from her neck. When she asked the question, she had an idea of what was going on. "Don't let that girl get in ya head," she said. She reached up and tried to fix Isis's hair but had her hand pushed away.

"It's too late for that, Aunt Camille!" Isis said, bumping Camille as she walked out of the room.

If Camille weren't pressed for time, she would have stayed to have a much-needed conversation. For now, trying to get the dope back was of the utmost importance. The future of her takeover plan was in jeopardy and depended on it.

Chapter 27

A full week went by, and there was still no Camille. Sarita was frustrated by it, mainly because Camille had most of Hassan's workers spooked. Nobody knew whether they'd be next on her "to-do list." The beef needed to be resolved before anybody could feel even remotely comfortable selling dope for Sarita. That in a sense caused a bigger problem, because as of the other day, Sarita was back in possession of most of the dope and had to move it in order to have her money ready for Torres.

"I've never seen this much dope in my life!" Rando exclaimed as he looked at the heroin in the storage unit.

Sarita didn't get all of the dope back from Camille, but there was enough to make her money back and still make a profit. Torres had given her a little more time to make a decision about working for him, so in the meantime, she had to at least make sure she had the re-up money.

"We gotta keep this secured until—" She was interrupted by her phone ringing. It was Dion, and she hoped there was some good news.

"He's awake," Dion said, looking over at Hassan lying in Sarita's bed. "And he's asking for you."

Sarita jumped into her car and drove out of the storage facility. It took her less than twenty minutes to get home, and as she entered her building, she began to think about how this conversation was going to take place . . . or if there was going to be a conversation at all.

"Yo, this is the last of it," Shooter said, walking into the kitchen with the book bag on his shoulders.

Out of all the heroin Camille had taken from Sarita, she was only left with a few kilos, which she cut up and sold. Shooter helped get rid of it. Since she had the connect, money was the only issue.

After the conversation they had at the club, Torres and Camille had another conversation over the phone, and Camille was supposed to meet up with him tonight. All he told her was to make sure the money was right, and that was exactly what she'd done.

"Here. That's another four hundred grand." She passed Shooter the money. She was supposed to get $1 million, but even though she didn't hit it, she was close enough to make Torres want to do business. "Y'all split that up," she said, pointing to the book bag Shooter brought in. "Oh, and I got something for you to take care of tonight, so make sure you cancel any plans you have wit' ya chickenheads."

The only reason she didn't pursue Sarita and her crew this week was because she was on a money mission. She definitely had to make up for the kilos of heroin Sarita took back. However, all of that changed. Camille came to the conclusion that all of her squabbles with Sarita needed to end once and for all. Tonight was going to be the night, and before it was all said and done, the city would belong to only one of them.

Sarita's bedroom was full of people when she walked in. Dion was there, Nasir, one of Sarita's personal security guards, Dr. Shobi, and another nurse from the hospital. Hassan was lying in the bed wide awake and breathing on his own. She looked into his eyes and didn't know how to read them.

"Can I have the room?" she asked everyone. She wanted to have whatever conversation she was going to have with Hassan alone. Nobody objected to it.

As Dr. Shobi was walking by, Sarita pulled out a manila envelope from her Gucci bag and passed it to him. "Thank you!" she said, then closed the door behind him.

The next thing Sarita pulled out of her bag was a gun: a ten-shot .40-cal. Hassan kept his eyes locked on her as she walked over to the side of the bed. Surprisingly, she grabbed his hand and put the gun in it. She then got down on her knees and placed both her hands on the bed.

"I think that before we have this conversation, you should have the upper hand this time." She really felt bad about almost killing him and was willing to accept any consequences behind her actions, even if that meant losing her own life. Tears filled her eyes just thinking about it.

Hassan lay there staring at her, and despite the fact that his injuries almost took his life, he couldn't fathom hurting a hair on her head. She was still his daughter, and he was still her father.

"I . . ." His voice was raspy, but he was going to make sure that he got it out. "I forgive you," he said, loosening his grip on the gun until it eventually fell onto the bed. "You're my daughter and I love you."

The tears poured out of Sarita's eyes. She couldn't believe that, after it all, he still wanted to be a father. Hassan had no hatred in his thoughts, no malice in his intent, but rather had pure love in his heart. Sarita never experienced anything like it, and now that she had, she never wanted to be without her father's love.

Camille sat at the kitchen table with a mountain of cocaine in front of her like she was Scarface. She'd been snorting all day, knowing that it was about to go down in a major way. She wanted to be numb to everything she planned on doing, especially when she saw Sarita face-to-face. Everything was on the line tonight, and she didn't have any intention of holding back.

"Yo! Y'all get ready!" she yelled out to Shooter, Big Chris, and Dice. She snorted another hit of cocaine, then looked over at Mega. "You too!" she demanded. "It's all hands on deck tonight."

The only reason Mega grabbed a gun from the table was because he didn't want to look weak in front of the fellas. He really wasn't built for this life, but he couldn't let it show. Any sign of weakness could mean the end of his reign before he could fully secure it.

"I have to go, but I'll be back," Sarita said, taking the gun off the bed and sliding it into her waistband.

"You know you don't have to do this," Hassan spoke in a low tone. "She's—"

"I know, Dad," Sarita cut him off. She didn't want Hassan to try to convince her to spare Camille's life, because she probably would do anything for him right now. She looked at Hassan, and for the first time, he smiled at her. "What?" she asked.

"You called me Dad."

If she had stood there any longer, she probably wouldn't have left. She walked over and kissed him on the forehead, then turned and walked out. As badly as she wanted to stay and kick it, she had business to take care of, and having her father on the brain wasn't going to be a good look.

"Take care of my dad," Sarita told Dion when she walked into the living room. "If you need anything, Shay will take care of it."

Shay, who was standing there listening, turned and looked at Sarita like she was crazy. "Shay is going with you! Don't play with me, Sarita!" Shay said.

Sarita could see in her eyes it wasn't even worth trying to talk her out of it.

Nasir was standing on the balcony when Sarita went out to join him. He tried to go back inside, but she stopped him by standing in front of the door. It was kind of awkward, because she really didn't know what to say to him. "I'm sorry for everything. I never meant to hurt you. And for what it's worth, I will always love you."

He looked off in the distance. He didn't want to hear those words come from her. At the present time, he was still confused about the whole ordeal, and his feelings were scattered all over the place.

Sarita wasn't about to press the issue. She reached up, pulled his head down, kissed him goodbye on his forehead, then left him standing on the balcony by himself.

"Come on, Shay. Let's go," Sarita said with only one thing on her mind: *kill!*

"Somebody left this for you," Detective Smith told Detective White.

White opened the manila envelope, and inside were two DVDs and a note that read:

A favor for a favor.

White looked at the DVDs, then walked them over to the conference room where he could view them. Smith was right behind him.

Dion was at the stage in her life when she had gotten tired of all the murders. Attempts on her and Hassan's lives, constantly looking over her shoulder, and worrying about people coming to do her harm had broken her. She wanted to bring an end to it all, and the only person she needed to get out of the way was Camille.

"Oh, shit! Are you seeing this?" White exclaimed as they watched the screen.

It was surveillance footage from Dion's home the night SK was killed, and it clearly showed Camille pulling the trigger and killing him. It was graphic and mind-blowing.

The second DVD was the sex tape Hassan made of Camille, depicting the consensual sex between the two and the murder that took place in the other room with Chuck.

"That's why he wanted to go to trial," White said. "He didn't want to send his brother to jail."

It was clearer now—at least pertaining to the rape—but the murder of SK was another story, one that neither detective understood at the moment. The one thing they could agree on was that finding out why Camille killed SK was top priority. She definitely had to answer for what went down.

Chapter 28

Nightfall came rather quickly, and Sarita parked her car under the el train on Sixtieth and Market Streets. The text Sarita had gotten from Camille an hour ago informed her that the location where they were going to meet had changed. The Fifteenth Street stop was where Camille chose.

Shay didn't think that it was a good idea and protested. But her protests only fell on deaf ears. Sarita had her mind set, and it didn't matter where they met up or who was around at the time. She was going to kill Camille. "Last chance," she said to Shay as she sat in the back seat of the car, putting her hair up in a ponytail.

Shay wasn't going anywhere but with Sarita.

The only way Sarita was going to get to the Fifteenth Street station was underground, which was by way of either the el train or the trolley car. She and Shay boarded the el train, and at 11:30 at night, there weren't many people on the train. "Just keep ya eyes open. She's not gonna be alone," she told Shay. "And watch out for SEPTA cops, too."

Sarita pulled her gun from her waistband and cocked it back slightly to make sure she had a bullet in the chamber, and Shay did the same.

"A'ight, here we go!" Shay said when the train went underground.

Fifteenth Street was only a couple of stops away, and it seemed like Sarita's heart began to beat faster and faster. She wasn't scared but more anxious.

"Doors are opening!" the announcement came once they got to Fifteenth Street.

It was like a ghost town when Sarita got off the train. Shay had switched cars and had gotten off a little farther back. Sarita let the train pull off before she pulled her gun out. She kept it down by her side as she made her way down the platform.

"I didn't think you would come," a voice echoed through-out the empty station.

Sarita looked around and spotted Camille standing across the tracks on the opposite platform. "Yeah, well, why don't you come over here?" Sarita yelled back.

Camille chuckled as she paced back and forth. "How about we talk for a minute? You know, like mother to daughter?"

Shooter walked into Sarita's condominium complex around 12:00 a.m. He wasn't worried that he was bare-faced, nor did he care about being seen. He strolled through the lobby like he lived there and even nodded to the security guard, who was making his rounds. Once on the elevator, he drew the seventeen-shot .40-caliber from his waist and held it by his side. There was already a bullet in the chamber, so there was no need for him to check.

When he reached his destination, he got off the elevator and looked up and down the hallway. He walked down the hallway with his gun in his hand, and the closer he got to Sarita's door, the faster his heart raced.

When he reached her door, he pressed his ear against it to see if he could hear anything. It was silent. He took one last look up and down the hallway, clutched the gun tighter in his hand, and knocked on the door.

"You know what's crazy? I can't believe you actually care about him. Ya dad was a piece of shit!" Camille yelled across to Sarita.

Looking up and down the platform, Sarita could see that there were a few people still waiting for the last train to come through. She wanted to close the gap between the two instead of shooting wildly in Camille's direction. "He was a better father than you were a mother!" she shot back. She was trying to make small talk as she conjured a plan to get closer to Camille.

"Yeah, well, he's dead now, and you can thank yourself for that!"

"He's still alive, you dumb bitch!" Sarita shot back.

"I'm always one step ahead of you. Don't ever forget that, Sarita!"

Dion took a bullet in the face as soon as she opened the door. Rando jumped up from the couch and drew his weapon. He managed to get off a shot before Shooter sent two hot slugs his way. Both hit Rando in the chest. Nasir raced from the kitchen over to his mother's lifeless body, unafraid of being shot.

The nurse who was coming out of the bathroom looked down the hallway and saw Shooter stepping over Nasir's and Dion's lifeless bodies. She dipped back into the bathroom, locked the door, and got into the bathtub.

The gunshots woke Hassan from his sleep, and by the time his eyes had adjusted, Shooter was standing at the foot of his bed, aiming the gun directly at him.

This was the moment Shooter had been waiting for—the chance to stand over Hassan and put a bullet in him. Without further delay, that was exactly what he did.

Pop!

The first bullet hit Hassan in his gut, knocking the wind out of him.

Pop! Pop!

The second bullet hit him in his chest, and the third hit him in his face right above his left eye.

Even still, Shooter wasn't satisfied. He ended up emptying the entire clip into Hassan, making sure that there was no way he would recover from this.

Shooter then tucked the gun in his pocket and walked out of the room.

"I told you, Sarita, I'm not the one you wanna play around with! I been out here in these streets way before you were born!"

Realizing Hassan was in a vulnerable situation, Sarita pulled out her phone. Her heart began to thump at the thought of it. She tried Dion's phone first but didn't get an answer. The landline was next, and she got the same results. She headed for the steps, all the while trying to call Rando's phone. Again, there was no answer.

Sarita could hear Camille yelling in the distance along with the last train coming. Camille thought that Sarita was going to leave, but she was actually coming straight to her.

As Sarita was walking through the tunnel to get to the other side where Camille was, she called Dr. Shobi's number, hoping that he'd pick up. He did. He answered the phone in a whisper as he hid behind the minibar.

"Dr. Shobi, where is my dad? Is he all right?"

"He's gone! Everybody's dead!" he whispered.

His words stopped Sarita in her tracks, but only for a split second. She stuffed her phone into her back pocket, then cautiously walked down the steps that led to Camille's side of the tracks.

Shooter got off the elevator and headed for the front door. A sense of relief came over him, and he felt good having gotten revenge for his friend's death. He could see the projects now: showing him love and giving him the utmost respect. He was going to be like the hero in the story.

As he crossed through the lobby, he looked for Mega, who should have been standing out in front of the condos. He wasn't there. The front desk clerk wasn't there and neither was security. Shooter could feel that something was wrong, but it was too late for him to do anything about it.

"Freeze! Don't fuckin' move!" Detective White shouted as he came from behind one of the partitions.

"Hands up! Hands up!" Smith also yelled as he came out of nowhere.

Shooter instinctively pulled the gun from his waistband, forgetting that he didn't have any bullets in it. He wasn't even able to raise the gun fully before Detective White fired his weapon. The bullet hit him in his stomach, dropping him to the ground. The gun he had in his hand fell to the floor. Before he could reach for it, White ran over and kicked it away from him, then placed him in handcuffs.

Mega was already sitting in the back of the squad car and was on his way to jail right along with Shooter.

This was all Camille's doing. She had given Detective White a tip, letting him know that a murder was about to take place. Her entire thought process consisted of her getting Shooter and Mega out of the way so she could take over the projects. And with those two gone, she knew she could manipulate her way to the top. She was vicious but very strategic. Unfortunately, she wasn't about to benefit from all the moves she'd made.

The train was pulling off as Sarita walked down to the platform. Surprisingly, Camille was still there, pacing back and forth with her gun in her hand.

"You know, it's not too late for us. We can take over the city. Just you and me," Camille said, stopping and facing Sarita.

Sarita didn't even consider what she was offering. She just wanted to get a little closer to her.

"Last chance," Camille offered, gripping her gun tighter. When Sarita didn't respond, she raised her gun and fired the first shot.

The bullet hit Sarita in her thigh, but she countered with several shots. One of the bullets whizzed by Camille's head as she slid behind a thick concrete beam. Sarita fired several more shots. When there was a break in the shooting, Camille took off running for the stairs.

***

Big Chris and Dice stood outside the entrance to the subway. When they heard the gunfire coming from the station, Dice tried running downstairs, but Chris grabbed his arm. "Nah, my nigga. Whatever's going on down there, just let it happen," he told Dice. "Let's see where she's really at."

Dice stood down, seeing the logic behind what Big Chris was saying. If Camille wanted to call shots in the projects, she needed to be able to handle herself like a big girl. Big Chris wanted to see if she would hit or miss. Whatever the case, Camille was on her own, and if she wanted to stay alive, she was going to have to show and prove her worth.

Sarita took off behind her, firing several more rounds at Camille as she ran up the steps. Camille turned around and attempted to fire several more shots at Sarita, but Sarita hadn't made it to the steps yet. When she turned back around in order to run down the tunnel, she ran right into Shay and froze as she stared down the barrel of her gun.

Unlike the last time they encountered one another, Shay didn't hesitate for a second. She squeezed the trigger, sending a hot lead ball straight to Camille's chest. The force from the bullet knocked her back down the flight of stairs, causing her to lose her gun during the fall.

Camille literally had the wind knocked out of her despite the fact that she had on a bulletproof vest. She lay on the ground and frantically tried to remove the vest so she could take in some air. But she never got the chance.

Sarita limped over and stood over her.

"So what? You gonna kill me too? You gonna kill me like you did your own father?" Camille yelled, hoping someone heard her. Her voiced echoed throughout the train station, but it made no difference because it was completely empty aside from the cashiers in their booths. But they couldn't hear anything.

Sarita looked down at Camille, and for the first time in her life, she felt like she was in complete control. Everything she'd been through in her life had brought her to this point. All the lies, all the pain, all the abuse—it all brought her here. This was the moment of truth, and for her, actually going through with killing her mother wasn't as easy as she thought it would be. Despite all her flaws, at the end of the day, Camille was her mother. That was how Sarita felt the moment she looked down at her mother, who had the fear of God in her eyes. She thought about not shooting her, but those feelings of guilt, remorse, and empathy were short-lived, and she came back to her senses. The time was now, the choice was made, and there was no turning back.

Sarita clutched the gun tighter, clenched her teeth, and pulled the trigger.

Pop!

Chapter 29

As Torres was just about to tee off on the fourth hole, Sarita came walking onto the golf course. She was dressed differently from what Torres was used to seeing her in. She was wearing blue jeans, a black hoodie, and Timberland boots. Her hair was in a basic ponytail. She had on no jewelry but sported a compact .357 Glock in her back pocket. She looked like a true dope girl.

"*Hola, mami!*" Torres greeted her, opening his arms to give her a hug. Over the last month, Sarita had to take some time off to get her mind right, and after everything she'd been through, Torres understood. "How are you?" he asked.

"I'm good. Just taking it one day at a time," Sarita replied.

"And have you given some thought to my business proposal?" Torres asked. He was still in need of someone to be the face of his drug operation on an international scale and still thought that Sarita was the perfect fit.

"I did, and I have to be honest with you, Torres. I'm not really ready for that type of responsibility. Plus, I just got into the game. I wanna try to conquer my city first before I move on to conquering the world."

She sounded sincere, and that was one of the reasons Torres liked her so much. The drug trade needed someone like her. "So what now? You out of the game?"

"I wouldn't say that." Sarita smiled. "I think I wanna switch it up a little. There's a wide-open market for cocaine in Philly."

He smiled at the thought. "And you want me to supply you?"

Sarita was through with the dope game. There was a lot of money on the table when it came to heroin, but she didn't feel like dealing with the headaches that came along with it. Cocaine was much easier, and there was still a lot of money involved. Plus, there was a huge demand for it. This was the new direction she wanted to go in, a direction Torres didn't mind accommodating.

"I'm going to Atlanta for a few days, and when I come back, we'll talk business," Torres said to her.

She smiled and began to walk off. "The streets are talkin', Torres!" she said.

"Oh, yeah? And what are they saying? I hope something good," Torres said.

"They say I'm up next!"